THE BAGGAGE CAROUSEL

David Olner

Published by Obliterati Press
2018

www.obliteratipress.com

ISBN: 978-1-9997528-1-1

Thanks to Nathan O'Hagan and Wayne Leeming for their enthusiasm and support. Top bananas, the both of 'em.

Thanks to Dolphin Dave for the photies. Cheers, head-head. And thanks to all the good, good people of Authonomy.

For Alan and Pat, Alfie and Lucy.

THE BAGGAGE CAROUSEL

Dan: Live From Heathrow

All the people on the way to paradise are angry because the check-in has opened late. I myself am calm for the first time in seven months, all my former rage now compartmentalised in a black box stored next to my sternum. The fifty-five minute delay was caused by a potentially extremist bag left in the vicinity of the desk. A robot was dispatched to remove it and now a cyborg is handling mine. This one wears too much foundation, but seems like a nice bloke. He clips a tag onto an appendage of my backpack as though it is a moorhen, whose migratory pattern he will study. Together, like bashful parents, we watch it shuffle through the curtain, readying for flight.

"May I see your hand luggage, sir?" he asks.

I hold it up.

"Any liquids in there, sir? Are you carrying anything sharp?"

Am I carrying anything sharp?

Only the bloodied shards of a fragmented heart that I will press to the carotid artery of the girl who smashed it. I should've put those in the big bag, really. It's always a rush job, packing for these suicide missions. I would imagine. This is my first.

It still worked out cheaper to buy a return ticket, though.

"No," I say.

He's flustered because the family who were at the desk before me had become abusive. Even the kids had a tokenistic stab, the youngest blowing spit bubbles malevolently and hurling a Tommee Tippee cup in the man's vague direction. I noted this and determined to use it my advantage.

"No need for that, is there?" I say, motioning over my shoulder at the troglodytes retreating to their Wetherspoons base camp. "Not like the plane's going to leave without us..."

"Exactly sir," he replies, momentarily taken aback by the deviation from our script. "I'm afraid not everyone's as patient as you."

He's got that right. I see a mote of humanity contaminate his clear eye as he considers my words and as he looks back up at me I feel that maybe I've done just enough to...

"I'm moving you forward a bit in the plane, sir," he says. "A little more legroom for the long flight."

"Thank you," I reply. "I wasn't expecting that at all."

I was weak and kind like him once. Not anymore. Look where it's got me. Even something as simple as an open front gate can be a come-on to a prospective burglar.

The gate opens and we steal aboard. Now I'm seated in the buffer zone between First Class and Economy. I wonder if I'll be forced to intervene in the event of an in-flight coup. It's a lot of responsibility, like when they put you in that seat next to the emergency hatch and part of your remit may include marshalling people towards the rubber slide of death.

It's not vastly different from economy. There are cut flowers in a glass vase in the bathroom – what a sad fate that is for any living thing. A little more legroom, as promised, video games on the seat-back screen, a dwarf bottle of wine marginally less acrid than the filth they serve in steerage. All around me, businessmen are perusing portfolios and pulling up projections as I play Tetris, everything tumbling into place for me finally.

I tap the screen to see the flight-plan. There are eighteen more hours to Sydney.

And Tommy.

And Amber.

Last, and foremost, Amber.

If she won't play with me, then I'll tear her Wendy House down.

I'm going to fuck her up, like she did me.

The creased suit next to me has put aside his documents and pulled a new book out of a WHSmith bag. While he reads the first few pages, he shuffles awkwardly in his seat, as though the words are nipping at him. A seasoned traveller, I have assumed dominance of the dividing armrest early – but during a tussle with the text, his elbow dashes against mine, almost creating sparks in the static air of the cabin.

"Sorry," he says, sighing and putting the book down over his leg, breaking its tender spine like a promise. "I just hate it when they don't start at the beginning."

"I know exactly what you mean," I say, hitting the video screen again to bring up an option marked *playback*.

SEVEN MONTHS EARLIER

From: danroberts@h–mail.com

To: amonsafari@whizzymail.com.au

RE: Departures

Dear Amber,

Please don't think me some obsessive type.

It's only been four hours since you left. It may seem overly keen that I'm emailing you already, but in truth, I can't think of anything else to do. Cape Town seems like the most mundane place in the world without you here. Occasionally, Table Mountain is folded away and, sometimes, the vuvuzelas play only "The Last Post".

You left earlier than I expected this morning and I didn't get a chance to say goodbye properly. As I recall, I just regarded you quizzically through the gauze of torpor and muttered a few unseemly syllables in your direction. Afterwards, I fell straight back to sleep and immediately dreamt that you were still lying next to me, with your dirty blonde curls tickling my nose. When I woke up sneezing, I was devastated to find you gone.

I also had a big lump on my forehead... you didn't whack me one in the night, did you?

In the dark of your departure, this once arresting city can no longer detain me. You were Cape Town to me. I've still got six hours before my flight – what am I to do? Maybe I could revisit our old haunts, go to Pickwick's Bar and sit on Our Couch like Greyfriars Bobby, quivering at footsteps, waiting for you to turn up. Squat there nursing a milkshake and fingering the holes in the battered upholstery in a doleful fashion, anticipating that hydroponic lamp smile of yours that can illuminate even the dingiest of dives, the shadiest *shebeen*.

No doubt as I languish there, monitoring the swinging saloon door like a nervous outlaw, the barman will catch me at it. Like any good Central Casting barman, he'll break off from polishing his shot glasses, sling his tea towel over his shoulder, and sigh wistfully. I'll be just another broken down sucker on Long Street, this bloke's seen it all before. What aspects of human behaviour could a barman on this Long Street of short, drunken lives possibly not have observed?

I'm limbo-dancing now. I really just wanted to use these hot and frozen hours to say that it's been a pleasure meeting and spending the last few days with you, Amber. And, yes, further to your demands, I WILL be seeing you in Sydney soon. I can call in and see my mate Tommy while I'm there. I just need to save for a while. Please bear with me.

All the best on your continuing travels, Amber.

Love,

Dan x

Dan: Undone

Shit.

Maybe I overdid it a bit with that last message. How come that only ever occurs to you once you've pressed 'Send', though? You never know how people will take these things. Sometimes there's such a fine line between sweet and sex-pest.

Four fucking hours. I must sound like a nutter. But I was thinking of her; wanted her to know that. I tried for endearing, ended up with unhinged. I tried to hide the real me, the one I always hope to leave behind in England each time I travel. It's the heavy coat I hang on the hook by the door. I'm never sure if I've managed it. I attempt to be a reformed character, a re-fried being, but maybe I've still got that faint whiff of the gallows about me. She'll sniff out that odour now, after I hid it so well during our time together. That email I just sent, the wrong kind of perfumed stationery.

I heard laughter and looked around the reception area, automatically assuming it was directed at me. It was only the bloke behind the pay-desk, though, chuckling to himself. He was eating chicken's feet, looking at up-skirt paparazzi shots on his greasy monitor. Tickled by Kim Kardashian's vagina.

He caught me looking at him. With one foot dangling from his mouth, he resembled an errant cat.

My last day in South Africa, and it's heaven, really, compared to the purgatory of my domestic life. Assuming you're a tourist, or part of a certain 9.2% of the population. I needed to get out of that dark little foyer and into the open. In the sudden absence of her smile, I hoped that everything would look better with a lick of sunshine upon it.

I foraged in my pocket for the last of the rands, finding instead the two little affixed koalas she gave me. I will carry them with me as a talisman, to ward off evil Customs officials on my Dubai connect. Them, I can never fool. They peg me for exactly what I am, some biro stain on the fabric of society.

Years ago, when I travelled in the U.S., I would be selected for additional security screening before every internal flight I took. I would be forced to stand in line with eleven swarthy men called Jorge, before being ushered into a tiny room to assume the Christ pose for a genital-strafing pat-down and bag swab.

For just a second, I would always think the manhunt was over. That they'd found me.

Dan: Patty

I've been robbed. I touched down in Dubai International Airport this morning. It's a massive, cruelly sterile building, like a big people hangar. I stood half-dead and brainless at the baggage carousel after a hellishly sleepless night spent watching movies spun off from phone apps. I stood unsteadily amongst all the holidaying ten-bob millionaires looking down their re-sculpted noses at me, awaiting the return of my backpack. I stood. And I stood.

In time, I was the only one still there. All the other passengers had picked up their designer bags full of designer clothes and fucked right off to their designer boutique hotels. I alone remained, watching the empty track roll around, a jilted John in a Mobius strip club.

Just as I was about to give up, there was a cracking sound and a dull thump from behind the rubberized curtain. Sickening noises that, where I'm from, usually correspond to a visiting Betterware salesman being blackjacked outside the council flats. Sure enough, a body was to emerge: the prone form of my backpack. A black, huddled mass vomiting up its own insides, akin to some African Ebola victim. One yellow flip-flop lolled from its gaping mouth like a feverish tongue, grotesquely licking at the skid-marked concourse.

My first thought was that my bag had committed suicide. An act stemming from deep-seated issues of low self-esteem, arisen from years spent playing servant to a cruel and uncaring master. These issues were brought to the fore when it endured ten hours trapped in a small compartment, forced into a dusty corner, enduring the haughty jibes of superior luggage items. Kid leather can be so cruel. I could almost hear its stifled cries:

"Make them go away! Make them go away!"

Closer inspection revealed malfeasance of a different kind. Verminous baggage handlers, disregarding the mammoth padlock affixed to the zipper, had instead simply prised open the zip's decaying teeth and raided its contents. The inside pocket had been opened and my camera was missing.

Some travellers come to love their backpack, and even give it a name. It always seems to be Bertha, though. Conversely, I've always despised mine. It's like lugging around an estranged Siamese twin: you want rid of it, but you know that it contains things vital to your survival. If I had previously given my bag a name, it would have been Twatface or Slobodan Milosevic.

But now my bag has been raped. It was held against its will in a dark place by a dark man who perpetrated dark deeds upon it. Strangely, I like my bag better now, and think little of the as yet undiagnosed havoc it has no doubt wreaked upon my lumbar region throughout all these field trips. Everyone hurts someone. My backpack is now no less damaged or dangerous than the rest of us.

Her new name is Patty Hearst.

Amber: In-flight Entertainment

That cloud over there looks a bit like my dentist.

I'm on the plane heading to Cape Town, looking out of the window because I'm bored by the choice of films. There's one where Samuel L. Jackson shouts a lot on one channel and one where Adam Sandler shouts a lot on the next. Samuel L. Jackson is a renegade cop but I haven't figured out what Adam Sandler is. He just seems to be a full-time prick. Why don't they star in one together? See who can shout the loudest and then the loser would agree not to make any more films.

I'm so over men with raised voices and the raised hands that follow. I wish I had someone to talk to. The old lady next to me is asleep, but an accidental-on-purpose elbow nudge soon wakes her up. I avert my eyes for a second; give her a chance to wipe the drool from her cardy shoulder. Then I turn back to her, beaming.

"Hi," I say.

"Hello," she replies, groggily.

Poor old thing. They really need their rest when they get to that age.

"Where are you off to, then?"

"Um, Cape Town," she says.

Makes sense. Stupid question, Amber.

"Travelling alone?" I continue.

"Yes, but my son's meeting me at the airport. He's not a black, though. He lives there now. He works in Equities."

"Oh, really? What's that then?"

These are key parts of my job. Being non-judgemental and pretending to care.

"I don't know," she, says, shrugging. "Are you on your own?"

"Yeah," I say. And she can go back to sleep now, because that's all I really needed to say; all I needed to hear myself say.

"Aren't you afraid?"

"Not anymore," I reply.

Her brow furrows and the resulting pressure closes her eyes again and makes her head droop forward. My training kicks in. I find her pillow on the cabin floor and gently move her into a reclining position. She doesn't wake up throughout this process. I am skilled at this movement. The Staff Nurse told me in a feedback session.

I feel tired myself now, all talked out from that lengthy back-and-forth and a little bit tipsy. I put the headphones on, switch to a music channel and recline my seat. Then I elevate it back up and take a big swig of white wine from the plastic midi on my tray-table. Then I recline it again.

That's better.

I probably shouldn't be drinking so much at altitude. But who's going to stop me now? Not Neville. Never Neville no more. Shit, I *am* drunk! No more of those sneaky little pencil lines he used to make on the wine bottles in the flat. He didn't know I knew about that. But he didn't know about the eraser I kept hidden in the kitchen drawer either.

My bestie Lozzer said that Neville was like salt. It always seems to be about food with her, eh? She said that Neville wasn't good for me but I needed him. But I don't need him now. I'm Amber, alone. A few days by myself in Cape Town to acclimatise and then I'll join my tour group and head out into the jungle. I'll sleep in a tent under the stars and fall asleep in no one's arms, listening to the chirping of birds and crickets, the snuffling of warthogs, the roaring of lions and...erm, whatever noise it is that elephants make.

Peace and quiet.

At last.

I lean forward. My drink is too far away. But I'm right where I should be.

5th February 2016

From: danroberts@h-mail.com

To: amonsafari@whizzymail.com.au

RE: Dubai

Dear Amber,

I'm in Dubai for my connecting flight home and I just don't get it. This place is weird. I've seen more culture in a pot of Munch Bunch yoghurt. I don't really feel this is an appropriate destination for backpackers, particularly not one on the bones of their arse at the end of their trip.

Everything gleams here except me. The dirty, travel-worn clothes hanging from my emaciated and burnt body bespeak my lack of bespoke tailoring. On golf courses around the city, tip-dependent caddies politely look away as millionaires hit mulligans, but the sand wedges in my fingernails are at once an emblem of my recent descent into savagery and a constant reminder of the unspoilt place I unrealistically hoped Dubai would be.

This place is like Vegas without the vices, and I suppose that is why it doesn't grip me. I walk around this city desolate and destitute, feeling like some doe-eyed, smudge-faced orphan with my nose pressed plaintively up against a cake shop window.

The hotels all have helipads, where guests gather to compare the size of their choppers. The doormen's top hats are customised with Velcro chinstraps lest the rotor blades blow them across to Abu Dhabi. There are always new openings for doormen in Dubai, but top hats are expensive. Inside these full, yet empty, buildings, white tigers prowl impatiently behind Perspex in the foyers, like stripy suited businessmen who missed their appointment. Lobbying for sport, looking put out about being kept in, flicking their tails dismissively at patrons they would consider perambulatory meals had they only encountered them in the jungles of Ranthambore. But the food here is far too rich for them.

In the miles and miles of malls, weekending start-up entrepreneurs and clam-baked Croydonites shop for ostentatious, tax-free talismans of their own avarice. They wince as their exposed, suckling-pig-pink shoulders rub against the more conservatively attired frames of royal entourages, there to seek out jewel-encrusted hoods for their liege's hawk. New and old money fold together in the same wallet, but circumnavigate around each other cautiously in the food courts. As true servants to the sovereignty sit demurely, having selected fruit smoothies and shawarma, all the sun-brittled Brits prostrate themselves in the hall of the Burger King, to tell each other whoppers over Whoppers and drown their taste buds with Coke Floats.

I stopped in last night, because it somehow wouldn't have felt right without you by my side. When seated now, my thigh feels naked without your tiny hand drumming upon it. My knee aches for a reassuring squeeze as you lean in towards me with a conspiratorial whisper. I ended up watching a *CSI: Miami* marathon on the telly. I finished up in that advanced state of solitude where you start shouting words of encouragement at the onscreen characters. The people in the next room probably thought I was being roughly sodomized by a man named Horatio.

I milled about for a while today (because if I stand still here, people will probably throw change at me) and now I'm back on my way to the hotel. I'll probably have a quiet one again tonight. I could probably have a quiet one in Basra now, it's been nothing but quiet since you left.

I sincerely hope that you're doing well and getting along with all the people on your trip. I miss you and I really do wish you were here with me, but I know you've got your own stuff to be doing and I respect that. No word from you as of yet, but no pressure. Drop me a line whenever you can.

Love,
Dan x

Dan: Home, Sweet Nursing Home

After my Dubai stop-over I returned home. Then I returned *to* the home. There to see my Grandma, the solitary flame flickering in the window denoting my absence, now ebbing too low to pose any real threat to the net curtains. The lady at reception looked panicked when I arrived. Her eyes kept darting from me to the carpark behind. I looked around and saw nothing. Maybe it was a soul fleeing.

"She was asking about you the other week," said the lady.

"Was she?" I asked. "What did she say?"

"She wanted to know if you'd painted the front door yet."

"Oh," I said, embarrassed. "I haven't."

She glanced up then, looked at me like she'd just found me at my grandmother's bedside with the life-support's plug in my hand.

"Mm-hmm," she said. "You shouldn't expect too much from her. She's already had a visitor today. She might be talked out."

My Grandma. Always the yapper.

"Who was the visitor?"

She flicked through the pages of a clipboard for a few minutes and then back to me.

"Don't know," she said, frowning.

But then, my Grandma probably didn't know who her visitor was either.

I got the feeling that the lady was hiding something from me, but at the same time, I wasn't sure if I wanted to know what it was. In truth, I was glad that someone had been looking in on my Grandma. It assuaged my guilt about being away for so long.

The one person who might truly have been pleased to see me didn't even recognise me. This came as no great surprise. When I was last in England, I would visit her every other day and she didn't recognise me most of the time then either. Sometimes, in the past, she has even thought I was her son, my father. But I didn't mind that so much; it was nice having him back around for a while, and an hour off from being me.

She looked older, more eroded, crumpled where she had once been pleated. I told her about some of the places I'd visited and the most I got was an occasional smile; a nod of non-comprehension. I had vainly hoped she would notice my absence, but her heart only grew weaker while I was away. I found all my sent postcards neatly stacked in the top drawer of a bedside cabinet and, in desperation, proffered them under her nose. Like she were a truffling pig, or some ageing bloodhound that might still be able to pick up my scent.

Eventually, I ran out of things to say. Becoming unaccountably angered by the artexed wall that seemed to engage her attention so raptly, I wheeled her into the TV room where antique people watched antique programmes. Another woman had been pushed in strapped to a bed, and a nurse was trying to work the controls to elevate her into an upright position. She pressed the wrong button and the entire bed began rising, up at an angle, heading towards the ceiling at an unseemly speed. The flustered nurse finally brought it to a halt when the alarmed woman's head was a few inches away from the hanging lampshade.

Don't go towards the light, I thought, and then immediately hated myself for thinking it.

Amber: Doing Men

A German named Peter puts his hand on my leg like it's Poland.

I'm *so* not down with that.

I've been in the hostel bar with him, his friends and two other Australian girls for the last few hours. So much for having character-building time by myself. So much for my vision quest. I rocked up at the place and then rocked back and forth on my dorm bed, waiting for someone to come and rescue me. I'm still not used to being on my own.

I'll get used to it.

I'll have to now.

We've been playing drinking games and each shot has amped up Peter's nerve. First, he started by doing that thing where he stares at my mouth when I talk. I hate that. It brings out my stammer and makes me think I've got spinach in my teeth. Which is funny, because I really loath spinach. In an ideal world, I'd like to see it reclassified as a plant. Then it was the accidental brushes, the annexing, the leaning in too close...

But not my leg. My minnie-moo lives at the end of it. I'm up out of my seat and straight to the bar. That same guy is still sat there on his own. Still totally oblivious.

A side note here: Sometimes guys stare at me and I really don't like it. Sometimes they try to play it cool and act like they haven't seen me. Not keen on that, either. But this guy sat here – he genuinely has no clue that I'm even present. I find that very annoying, especially when he's completely engrossed in reading a laminated sign about fire evacuation procedure.

I'll make an effort. Just this once. Good going on the relinquishing men thing, Amber! At the very least I made it through the flight without sucking anyone off. But I'm only going to talk to him for a little bit. Maybe he's lonely. Plus, he might be a good guy to get on side if there's a fire. I order some bogan cocktail from the barman and then sidle closer.

"How ya goin'?" I ask.

He turns. He's alright looking. Nothing to Skype home about. He's got nice arms. Not too big. Not big enough to really hurt me.

"I'm okay, thanks," he says. He's got a funny accent. Irish, maybe. "How're you?"

"Good, thanks," I say and then the flowing conversation cuts short and he's back looking at that bloody sign again.

"Alright there on your own?" I ask, feeling a strange urge to irk him.

"Fine," he says. "If you're a stranger alone at a bar you usually find that someone will start talking to you before too long. The unfortunate part is that they're usually the type of people who talk to strangers at bars."

"Ah, yeah? What type of people are they, then?"

"The mentally infirm, mostly."

A piss-ripper. Just what I need. I'm not sure if he's joking or insulting me, but I do know that I'm too drunk to deal with it right now. I felt okay when I was seated and fending off Germans but as soon as I stood up the floor kind of lunged at me. I'm considering that this bloke might be an even bigger toolbox than the one I've just swerved when a great big smile hijacks his face and he speaks again.

"What's your name?" he says.

"Ama...Amber." Nearly ballsed that up, there.

"Dan," he replies, extending a hand.

"Nice to meet you, Dan. Y'know, you're more than welcome to join us..."

We both look in the direction of the table and I expect to see Peter glaring back at me. But instead, he's watching one of his mates, who's coughing and spluttering with what looks like semen coming out of his nose.

"White Russian," I explain to Dan, as though that makes what we're looking at somehow acceptable.

"But what's that stuff coming out of his nose?"

"They're playing drinking games," I tell him, laughing, wondering exactly how I became spokesperson for this gang of lunatics.

"Ah," he says. "I don't drink. Without the drinking, it's just a game. I don't care too much for games."

Fair one. Everyone hates games. They're just no fun at all.

"How come you don't drink?" I ask, then realise he'll probably despise that question. I know, because I was a vegetarian for three weeks once and I only started eating meat again when I got tired of people asking me why I didn't. And because I kept dreaming about gammon. And because Lozzer kept forwarding photographs of pies to my phone.

"My mother used to drink," he says.

Whoa! A guy with Mother Issues. How truly rare.

"I'm sorry," I say. "Did she pass?"

In the hospital, we're taught that as a polite way to say "die."

"She definitely passed," he responds. "But she's not dead."

No small talk with this one, eh? I think I like him a bit, even though he's doing my head in. I feel like I'm on a blind date with The Riddler.

"Okay, well...bye," I say, because I can't think of anything else to say.

"Bye, Amber."

He stays sat there, but somehow, he's gone before I am. As I move away from the bar, carrying my bright green drink before me like a lamp, I can't resist calling one last thing over my shoulder.

"I think it's great," I shout, "how you manage to keep yourself so cheery without alcohol!"

Advantage, Miss Shaughnessy! I re-join my table stoked and sit at the other end from Peter who's peering over at me like I fucked his cat. I don't care. I'm looking elsewhere. From this vantage point, I can see my strange new friend's back. His shoulders are shaking. I'm not entirely sure if he's laughing or crying.

Dan: Character Based Rant #1

I like it when you first get back from your travels and catch up with whatever friends you have left and the one present member of your family. I live in a small Northern town full of unadventurous people, who think that you fall off the edge of the world if you venture out past Rotherham. However, once a year they stop throwing stones at the overhead planes for long enough to board one, and make their yearly sojourn to Magaluf or Falaraki.

Once there, they spend a week sitting in Lineker's bars eating Full Monty breakfasts washed down with adoptive English Stella Artois. They use this to swill away morning-after pills and memories of the previous evening's lurid sexual misadventures like an abattoir worker hosing arterial cow's blood down into a drain.

Yesterday, by the pool, they had their eye on some Scandinavian, leered at them through Ray-Bans that also bluntly obscure pointed lechery. But the rest of Europe has been briefed about the English; they view our scabby little island as we would view a research centre for rabid badgers. All too painfully aware of the English people's capacity to turn from Mogwai into Gremlin after midnight, the Scandinavians made their excuses after the evening barbeque, dumping their last proffered shot of Sambuca into a terracotta jardinière. They left the English to fall into the pool and each other's beds; left them to settle for the night.

Back at the breakfast table, the English instead knock flakes from their peeling noses onto their eggs like pepper. Then they say:

"Hot though, innit? *Muggy.* Didn't sleep a wink. I was sweating like a glassblower's arse all night."

"It's them donkeys I feel sorry for."

"No, I don't use sun cream; I burn first, then I go brown."

"This bacon tastes funny."

"By, those Geordie lads are looking a bit rough this morning."

"The bloke sat on his own with the book? Coloured chap? London, I expect."

"Ooh, the hypnotist was a bit blue last night. No need for it, what with the kiddies still being about. It was a midnight show, mind."

"No, I'm Sky-plussing *X-Factor*, do you know who went out?"

"S'nice to be away though, innit? Takes your mind off home."

So, by contrast, when I return from my travels I'm regarded with suspicion and mistrust:

"You went *where*?"

"What did you want to go *there* for?"

"They don't even put their bog-roll down the toilet *there*, do they?"

I bite my tongue and explain that no, they didn't put their bog roll down the toilet in Angkor Wat, but if you can get beyond that limitation, it does have other charms. I go on to detail them and they remain unimpressed, until I mention that *Tomb Raider* was filmed there:

"Tell us more of the Outland, minstrel."

Thus, I hold court in Working Men's Clubs and Miner's Welfares, programmed into the schedule between the weekly asylum-seeker lynching and the meat raffle, weaving tall tales of far-flung lands. I am indulged more by the older ones, because I am and always will be 'Alfie's young un', some twenty years after my father's death. But after a while, even they've had enough of me:

"Who does he think he is?"

After all the hype and hoopla dies down around me – after they are satisfied I have returned as neither a spy nor a Scientologist – I slot right back into the familiar holding pattern of my old, other life, back into hibernation until I've amassed enough money for the next trip. So now, all the sights and sounds of Africa will self-incinerate like over-exposed film stock. Lions and elephants crushed back into the dulled stardust they began from.

Soon everything will be grey again.

14th February 2016

From: danroberts@h–mail.com

To: amonsafari@whizzymail.com.au

RE: Away

Dear Amber,

Happy Valentine's Day! I wish I had a geographical fix on you so I could send you a card, some of those chocolates shaped like seashells, a fruit basket, a white ostrich feather, an eight-track tape of love songs, a bottle of Blue Nun, luncheon vouchers...whatever it is that people are supposed to send each other on this day. As you can no doubt tell, I'm a little bit rusty with the whole concept of Valentine's Day. I can't remember the last time I even sent a card. There's just never usually anyone I care about enough. Usually.

Until you came along.

There have been occasional dalliances over the last few years, but they never really went anywhere. Because I was always going somewhere. Getting mixed up with a girl always seemed to me to be tantamount to burning my passport.

In the small town where I live, most blokes' lives follow the same trajectory: they grow up, marry some girl they went to school with, and then settle into a home a couple of streets away from their mum's house to raise children who will repeat the same cycle. They pop back round there to drop these kids off in the half-term holidays, or borrow a Pyrex dish on occasion. Mum still worries the competition's not feeding her little soldier right, so she slyly fills it with cauliflower cheese until it almost cracks.

That's most blokes' mothers. My mother isn't around the corner. I don't know where she is, nor do I care. I doubt that she owns anything as practical as a Pyrex dish, but if she did, it would probably be filled *with* crack.

It's been a while since I sent a Mother's Day card too.

If there is just one true soulmate for every person in this world, then how come they always seem to live in the same town? It's all a bit too convenient, don't you think? Statistically, it's far more likely they'd be in China. It seems like some people might just be making do, settling for settling. A cautious man when conferring affection on females (thanks again, Mum) I always adhere to The Hays Code when it comes to matters of the heart, keeping one hiking boot firmly on the ground at all times.

Again, until you came along.

It's awful to say this, but when I'm overseas I never miss anyone, neither friends nor family. Not even my beloved Grandma, who did her level best to raise a surly, withdrawn youth with one parent in the ground and another in the wind. But now I miss you. It's fine that I haven't heard from you yet; I want you to enjoy yourself. Fuck homeward, angel. Stay out for as long as you can, and speak to me whenever you get the opportunity.

Nothing's wrong here, but at the same time, nothing's quite right. Thinking of you, I'm reminded of when I used to keep a pen behind my ear all day at work and then when I returned home it would still feel like it was there, even hours later. As I write that, I know that it's not the most romantic analogy, but my first choice involved amputees, so I had to have a re-think.

I was never before even an overly tactile person. Never saw the point of touching people, unless it was in self-defence. But when you and I walked the streets of Cape Town together, and your dainty little hand would seek out my clammy, meaty paw, it would feel as elemental and true as a dovetail joint coming together.

I feel that we are a good, if unlikely, fit. Remember how I used to like to hook my thumb into your belt loop as we sat together? It felt so snug and right there, because it kept you close to me. I hope, soon, I will get the chance to house it there again.

Happy Valentine's Day, Amber. Even if I don't hear from you straight away, today I would like you to know that, wherever you may be in the world right now, you are always near to my thoughts, and never too far away from my heart.

Love,
Dan x

Amber: Prison Break(fast)

Breakfast at a hostel is like one of those scenes in a prison movie where the greenhorn con doesn't know which table to sit at. Unlike in those movies, I find it's always best to avoid the French. They blow smoke in the marmalade and stare at my tits. The Australian girls are still in bed and I think, for today, we can also rule out the Germans. Even with a wicked hangover, I can sense Peter's look from across the room, cold enough to freeze warts.

Where is my wily old lag? In the prison films, there's always a wily old lag to show the newbie the ropes. I'm looking for that guy Dan, and I don't even know why.

There he is. In the corner. Sat alone, unsurprisingly. A secure wing, far removed from Gen Pop. No known gang affiliations.

"Morning!" I say. I'm trying for jaunty but sounding deranged as I approach his table. My voice comes out funny because he's the first person I've spoken to today – apart from telling someone in my dorm to "roll the fuck over!" at about 4am.

"Morning, Amber," he says, a breakfast-appropriate smile on his face.

"Mind if I join?"

"No, I don't mind."

Gosh, thanks for that ringing endorsement.

"You're feeling okay today?" he asks, as I settle in. There's a slight insinuation in his tone that sends me back into my archive of last night's events, looking for clues.

404 File Not Found.

"Good, thanks," I bluff, and then look down to see that I'm spreading jam on a sausage.

"What are you up to today?"

"I'm going to prison."

That's spooky, I was just rattling on about prisons!

"You do have that look about you," I think. And then realise I've said it out loud.

Oopsie.

"Evidently, I'm a recidivist," he says and I laugh politely to cover my foul-up, even though I have no idea what that word he just said means. But it sounds like something clever and funny, and I know men like it when you laugh at those kinds of things. Especially when they said them.

Damn. I keep forgetting that The New Me doesn't crave the approval of men anymore. Move to strike that last thought from the record!

"Robben Island," he adds and then, seeing the blank look on my face, elaborates further. "Where the ANC prisoners were held?"

Still nothing.

"Nelson Mandela?"

Ah. I do know who Nelson Mandela is. He met the Spice Girls and Naomi Campbell counts him as a close personal friend. He's a man who has suffered a great deal in his life.

"Can I...can I come with you?" I ask.

"I don't see why not," he says.

Jeez, sweep a girl right off her feet, why don't you, Englishman?

Dan: Back on the Sausage Roll

Today I went to sign on. I had an early appointment and arrived first thing, before the Jobcentre had opened. The frosted and forgotten men already gathered outside stamped their feet against the insidious chill of a February morning. They rolled matchstick-thin cigarettes with hands still calloused from servitude to the industries that had long since discarded them. Neutered pit moggies, whose redundancy pay-offs had long since blown away like coal dust. Like coal itself. Steelworkers who had been replaced by plastic robots. All that was really missing was an oil drum brasserie on which to roast skewered rats. The Mole People of the New York subway system call them track rabbits.

When the Jobcentre opened, the younger generation seeped through the door like pus. Fashionably late – they don't like the cold so much. They think that outdoor toilets are an old folk's story, and that backyard coal-scuttles were once kennels for photosensitive dogs. It's funny how they're always on time when they pick up their methadone scripts, though.

They left their electric blankets on whilst they went to sign on and they will duck back under the covers when they return. They wore the caps of baseball teams they don't support, located in cities they'll never visit. They chewed gum and thrust their hands inside their tracksuit bottoms without shame. From there, they pulled out phones and updated their Facebook status as they waited.

Paul Hutchinson is...signing on.

When called, they gave the clerks doubly negative attitude:

"I never got no letter. Swear down, I never got it. Swear on me babby's life. It's not my fault. I best still get me money on time. This place is a joke."

Nobody laughed. While they waited, the older men kept busy by banging their heads against the noticeboards that taunted them with employment opportunities they were entirely unsuitable for. Meanwhile, the young ones headed straight to the couch to slouch, now using their phones again to listen to grime music through a dirty earpiece. With those in place, they scanned the room blankly, looking like inept Training Scheme Secret Service agents. These appointments are a massive chore to them, a ten-minute working week that impinges on their uncivil liberties. I stood between these two groups and I had no idea which one I belonged in. I read a pamphlet about benefit sanctions to pass the time. Welcome back to The Little Society.

Every time I come back from a trip, I have to go through a familiar rigmarole. I am assigned a clerk to work through the same form, in which I must answer ridiculous questions concerning my alien status. For the record now, and in case you ever wondered, let me categorically state that no, I was not evacuated from Montenegro after the 1979 earthquake. It's a bind for me to have to prove citizenship of my own country each time I return to it, but I always remain civil and polite, if only to distance myself from the gobshite hoodlum mouthing off at the next cubicle along.

I was batted about the system for most of my adolescence. I am all too well aware of the power government-appointed officials have to give and take away. I remain polite at all times. I address the clerk by the name on their tag. They respond positively to that, as do waitresses and dogs.

Today I had Karen. She wore a razor bob haircut like a helmet to protect her in the arena of the unemployed, and applied chap-stick intermittently as a barrier cream. She asked me where I had been on my travels.

"Africa," I said.

"Ooh, I watched a film about that last night," she replied.

"Oh really, what was it called?" I asked.

"Madagascar."

She then asked me if I had been to Madagascar, and when I responded in the negative, she seemed disappointed that I had no stories of talking lions to regale her with.

The tedium of that form set aside, Karen asked me what sort of work I am looking for. I told her my field and she fed it into the computer. No matches. Do I have a back-up plan? No matches. Third time lucky? No matches. I was summarily sworn into the ranks of the unemployed, I laid my hand upon my benefit card and made a solemn pledge that I would do three things each week to expedite employment. Third time lucky.

"I bet you wish you hadn't come back, don't you?" Karen asked in closing, a question as redundant as I apparently now am.

Originally, I was supposed to be returning to my old job, but that didn't work out. I was employed at a clothing warehouse in the next village down from mine, and they had agreed to let me take a sabbatical to go to Africa. However, in my last week of work, people began dropping off sick with flu. I went to see my manager, herself recently recovered from the illness, to broach the notion of finishing ahead of my period of notice to avoid contracting it.

Managers are like social workers: they always like to give it the large talk about how you can come to them with any problem and they will work together with you to arrive at a solution. I thought it was a reasonable concern of mine to be worried about the possibility of contracting a highly contagious disease, just ahead of flying to a continent with a generally more basic healthcare system than one's own and an alarmingly high mortality rate. I felt my duty of care for others alone would enable me to get an early finish.

My manager disagreed. She was a large-headed, brutal looking woman, whose eyes would roll right back into her head when she became stressed. When I voiced my proposal, she looked like a medium receiving a spirit.

"You could just as easily contract flu from someone you walk past on the street," she said.

"I suppose that's possible," I said. "But I think it's more likely I could contract it working for eight and a half hours a day in a confined area alongside people who had already had it, or who currently have relatives at home who are suffering with it. Not that I'm a doctor."

Considering this, she modified her theory somewhat:

"You could catch it from going into the shop," she said.

"But I don't need owt from the shop," I replied.

"Now you're just being stupid."

It had been a lacklustre debate prior to that comment. We both knew I was walking and were just dancing around each other, trying to determine how soon. But I really don't like it when people call me stupid. A foster parent called me that once, albeit in a much more heated exchange. I knocked him through a flat-pack wardrobe that we were assembling at the time, and then went after him with a screwdriver.

This in turn bounced me out of the system and back to my Grandma's house. A tad ungrateful really, as the wardrobe was supposed to be for 'my room.' But my room was twenty-six miles down the road, not in the house of some ginger stranger with a low sperm count and Airfix models in his study. And puncture marks in his thigh.

I tried to articulate all this to my employer, but words wouldn't carry easily through the clenched teeth of my war-mask. I got that bad old feeling again. All that was emanating from my brain was hot blood, coursing down my veins and towards my fists, now also clenched. Such a big face on that woman. Such a wide-open target. But I've never hit a woman in my life. Only men, by default.

Dissolve.

After the police came, I complied with their instructions to the letter and left the premises. They even gave me a lift. I was pleased with the outcome of the meeting. I was aiming for finishing at the close of the working day, but even after the formalities down at the station, I was on a bus home at 11.46am. No charges were pressed, although my last pay packet came back a little light.

There's a lot to be said for the careful application of mindful violence. I would assume a reference is out of the window though. Gone the same way as most of my former employer's office furniture.

On the way up to the bus stop, I bought myself a celebratory sausage sandwich from the bakers. But, ever mindful of my now former employer's entreaties, I didn't dare venture into any shops.

I'm not stupid.

INCIDENT REPORT
COMPLAINANT: Dan Roberts
LOCATION: Fort Lauderdale, USA.

I was in a Howard Johnsons restaurant performing an autopsy on the remains of a toasted cheese sandwich. My waitress, Beth Pleased-To-Serve-You, passed by.

"Was everything okay with your meal, sir?"

"I didn't like it," I said. "The cheese was plasticky. What kind of cheese was it?"

"That's American Cheddar, sir," she replied.

Uh-oh. Proceed With Caution. Your room at the Guatanamo Bay Hilton is almost ready, sir. Waterboarding starts by the pool at three.

"I'm sure it's very nice. I think it's just not to my taste," I said, diplomatically; the Kofi Annan of the coffeehouse.

Beth smiled and was about to respond when another voice cracked through the room like a nail bomb.

"Hey!"

Here we go. I looked over to the adjacent booth and saw a young bloke leaning across, pinning his bikini-clad girlfriend's bare back against the sticky vinyl with a ham hock elbow.

"You got a problem with America, guy?"

I'm in a cartoon world. There's a bubble above my head that says "SIGH!"

"Obviously I don't or I wouldn't be here," I replied. "I was just telling Beth here...in a *private* conversation, by the way, that I didn't care too much for the cheese."

"Oh yeah?"

"Yeah."

"So, like, how's the cheese where you come from?" he asked.

I thought about this for a moment. Flashed on an absurd image of yokels breaking their necks to chase a ball of the stuff down a hill. Considered that if cheese were as valuable a trading commodity as oil, England might still rule the world.

"It's actually really good," I declared.

"Oh yeah? Maybe you should *actually* go home then. Maybe you shouldn't *actually* come to other people's countries and *actually* malign their cheeses."

Malign their cheeses? Jesus. I pushed the plate away from me and leaned forward across the linoleum; across the Atlantic.

"Take it easy, guys," said Beth, nervously. "This isn't Denny's."

I smiled at her and addressed the imbecile anew.

"How do you see this ending up?" I asked. "Do you really want to get into a fight over a toasted cheese sandwich?"

He did. That's how it usually starts: when stupid people are too stupid to even realise that they're being stupid. He was a big fucker when he stood up as well. One of those frat boy, Nautilus machine, acquaintance-rape types. *I tried to fight him off*, remarked the plaintiff, breaking down in tears, *but he was just so strong.*

I'm not a big man myself. More of a sinewy type, like a shithouse rat. To level the playing field, I whacked him across the back with a stool as he left the restaurant before me. A sneaky move, but trickier than you might think when the place has a revolving door. He careened through it at such a speed that I had to wait for the door to slow down before I could get out. When I arrived on the street, he was pitched forward, wheezing like a pigeon fancier. A cursory boot to the arse sent him sprawling forward and I heard the disheartening crack of his nose as he went flat on his face.

Oops. I felt so bad about it that I rolled him over and tried, mostly unsuccessfully, to lug him into a sitting position against a mailbox. He kept sliding to one side, looking like a Guy Fawkes dummy on a paintball course. There was a deep cut across the bridge of his nose and he was still coughing and spluttering. Blood was seeping down onto his Hollister polo shirt, as though the seagull was having a heavy period.

I turned back towards the restaurant and through the glass I could see his girlfriend babbling into her smartphone. Scrambling the police, the coastguard, possibly Immigration and Naturalization. Next to her stood Beth, holding her laminated menu up against her chest like it was Kevlar. It occurred to me then that I hadn't paid for my sandwich. I mouthed a word at them both and started to run.

Sorry.

Dan: The World Wide Web

Still no word from Amber. Is she done with me now? Is she, like, *so over me*? I am but a tacky souvenir, lost in her baggage. I am a SeaWorld key fob.

I wouldn't blame her for discarding me. They all do, eventually. Even I grew tired of myself years ago. Before her, it was only ever the thought of travel that kept me going, compelled me to prise my head from the pillow each morning. Now, I'm back home, running on empty again.

Maybe I should wait it out. Maybe her trip hasn't pulled up to anywhere with internet access yet. Maybe they're still rough-camping out in the jungle. I went on one of those overland trips myself once, through Asia. That didn't always run so smoothly. It's a different mindset from backpacking. The backpackers you meet in the hostels have their little eccentricities and quirks but on the whole they conform to a certain template – idealistic, left-leaning, romantic slacker types, drifting from job to job and place to place.

Overland jaunts, however, tend to attract the more focused, careerist types. They want to see all the same things that the backpackers do, but can't quite bring themselves to completely relinquish control and embrace the chaos of travel in the same way. So the Overland excursion provides just enough form and structure.

Most of the people on my Asia expedition were IT consultants in the grip of mid-life crises. Downsized, recently divorced, ransacked nest syndrome with the youngest kid just recently decided that they hate them – there was always some sort of impetus behind their decision to travel. A perfect time in their lives to cut loose a little bit, and yet, sadly, years of institutionalization had left them unable to do so. Try as they might, they could not fight their programming.

We'd be travelling in a 4x4 through the majestic splendour of the Wadi Rum desert or some such place and they'd be sat in the back oblivious to it, holding endless round table discussions about finding better, more ergonomic ways to store our sleeping bags in the truck's hold. On one occasion, we pulled up outside a beautiful caravanserai in Syria and the driver gave us a little potted history of the place before letting us out of our rolling lobster pot. Eleventh century, medieval, Cradle of Civilization, etc, etc... the group all listened to the speech dutifully and when he'd finished the driver asked if there were any questions:

"Is there anywhere around here with internet access?" one of them asked, without any trace of irony.

Back then, everyone needed internet access because everyone was working on blogs. They would piss away full days in measly little internet cafes writing blogs about all the things they could be seeing if they weren't pissing away full days in measly little internet cafes writing their blogs. Always more given to looking through Windows than looking through windows.

I've developed an ardent hatred of these blogs and group travel emails ever since. You can be just minding your own business at home and one of these Round Robin messages pops up to ruin your day – some arsehole you once shared a greasy pizza with in a Tallinn hostel, now slavering on about how they've just dined on freshly caught sea bass round the village chief's house in the Cook Islands.

That's great, you think. *I just watched Coronation Street with three bars on the fire. I accidentally put the green bin out instead of the black bin the other day and I haven't had a useful erection since August. Do you really want me to hijack your attention with the minutiae of my life too? Because that's where I'm at right now.*

LOL.

Smiley face.

These are the same kind of people who would probably upload their CAT scan images onto Facebook. Thumbs up. Five people like this. Is there nothing in your life you would like to keep to yourselves? If a tree falls in the woods and no one is around, well then that's bad news for the tree, but it's several million less Tweets about it that the world is spared.

I typed Amber's name into the computer today, and it came up with her Facebook profile. She looked really beautiful in that postage stamp sized image. It'd probably be easier for me to contact her if I was on Facebook, but I'm not a member. I was briefly, but I was never too keen on the idea of people tracking me when I went away. For me, getting away from it all has always been more about getting away from *them* all. All those social networking sites are basically just bulletin boards for imbeciles. Half-witted attention seekers, constantly updating their status to show you photos of what they just had for elevenses, or grandly announcing plans to scratch their own arse.

As a social experiment once, I set up a bogus Facebook page. I selected a generic name for my imaginary subject. Rob Danson. Chances are you've met a Rob Danson at some point in your life, and even if you haven't you'd probably think you had if one approached you. I deliberately made my Rob Danson a cipher – no photographs, no personal details, and then sent out friend requests to a random cross section of people. Most people accepted these requests right off the bat. Some would ask questions first:

"Have we met?"

"Do I know you?"

"Are you the Rob from the next-door chalet at Val D'Isere?"

To each of these queries I (as Rob Danson) would reply: No. Half of these people still accepted the request anyway. The last time I looked at Rob Danson's home page he had more than twice as many friends as me. The fucker didn't even exist. It was at that point I abandoned my experiment and my own Facebook page, as all it seemed to be doing was reiterating my own insignificance.

Dan: Oh

Travel can warp the mind. In Mozambique, I undertook a typically hellish, thirteen-hour bus journey from Maputo to Villanculos alongside a Netherlander named Gabriel. We arrived at our destination exhausted and I asked my new friend how it was that just sitting on a bus all day could tire one out so.

"It's because you are essentially a biped," he said. "Designed to walk der earth without mechanized assistance. Technological advances in transportation now enable you to travel to destinations much faster, but your primitive brain is still only conditioned to receive visual images at walking speed. A day spent on der bus with new imagery filtering in at breakneck speed is a sensory overload to der brain. Der brain thus requests sleep in order to contextualize and process this new data."

"That's what I thought," I said.

Thirteen hours on the bus. He comes out talking like Stephen Hawking and I come out walking like him.

Obviously, Gabriel had smoked a lot of pot in his time. He also told me that "Pinocchio" was a Christ allegory and that I shouldn't eat peanuts at night because they would lie on my chest. I didn't really understand what that last point meant, but the biped theory at least made sense to me. Lots of backpackers come off as slightly vacant, waiting-for-the-mothership types, and now there appeared to be some justification for that. Constantly on the move: always new places, new people, new customs, new currency, new languages to contend with every few days...

I try to avoid communal chambers because I'm borderline sociopathic. But I once took an overnight train from Paris to Madrid. I shared the couchette compartment with two elderly Italians and a young Nigerian lad. The Italians didn't speak a word of English but I managed to exchange a few basic pleasantries with the Nigerian. I don't think he'd ever been on a sleeper train before; when I showed him how to pull his bunk out of the wall he regarded me incredulously, as though I were a warlock.

Back, shaman, back!

The compartment was intoxicatingly warm. That, combined with the gentle, unhurried undulation of the train, soon conspired to send me into a deep sleep. When I later woke, half-snoring, half-laughing, I had no idea where I was. The Nigerian was staring down at me quizzically from the upper bunk, but he was a very black man and all I could make out was a pair of widened eyes glaring at me through the rumbling night. For those few waking moments, I thought I was in a woodland copse and was certain that he was an owl.

"Where the fuck am I?" I asked.

"You are on the train," he replied.

"Oh," I said, and immediately fell back to sleep.

I had a similar moment of clarity again today. I was thinking about Amber – as I do every day. I was missing her– as I do every day. I was worried about her – as I have been every day. I wanted to see her pretty face again, so I typed her name into the computer. Once again, her Facebook profile came up. What better place could there be to look for a face?

Her old photograph had been replaced with a more recent snapshot. She was frolicking with her new friends from the Overland tour, oblivious to the concern that her lack of communication has engendered in me.

"Oh," I said, finally waking up.

Dan: Good Hiding

When I was on that train to Madrid, I dreamt of my late father for the first time in years, remembered myself as a young child playing hide and seek in the house with him. I would always hide in the airing cupboard. It felt like the rumbling heart of the house. I would always hide in the airing cupboard because I secretly wanted to be found. I was then small enough to fit on the middle shelf, cocooning myself in amidst the clean, soft laundry; a snug and smug Sultan in a Bedouin tent of bath towels.

I would hear my father enter the bathroom with his theatrical, trip-trapping footsteps. Usually he was lighter on his feet, possessing the familiar, Popeye-like build of most colliers. A cut and shut; a minotaur's torso atop the legs of an accountant. Funnel shaped, like a tornado, genetically designed to tear chunks out of the ground. And pick up the occasional cow, like my mother.

Years before, he had knocked one of his front teeth out in an accident down the pit. As he yanked open the cupboard door, he would slide his false tooth down with his tongue and leer in at me with an accentuated and exaggerated menace. He would pull me from the shelf and rub his grizzly, stubbled cheek against mine until I begged for surrender between bursts of hysterical, hyperventilating laughter.

When I awoke he was dead again and I was once more lost.

Amber: Nelson Mandela the Smoking Nazi

Dan's one of those people who actually *listens* to what the tour guide says. I try, but after a while, they all sound like that teacher from Charlie Brown. Not only that, but he also wants to touch everything. Like if the guard – sorry – guide, says something about the materials that make up a wall, Dan will go over and stroke it.

He's kind of a freak.

And! And! And! He asks *questions*. I swear the only questions I've even asked a tour guide are the two basics

1. What time is lunch?

2. When will this end?

My only interaction with the guide is accidental. We're out in the prison yard and he's giving it the heavy talk about all the men who were falsely imprisoned, tortured and ultimately died within the building's walls. I lean over to Dan.

"Dunno about that," I say, "but I am fucking *dying* for a cigarette!"

It's the first counterfeit smile I've seen from Dan, and I feel short-changed and cheapened. Way to misjudge the mood, Amber. Ya silly bitch. On top of that, the tour guide hears my remark. It's about as well received as the time I accidentally broke wind in Auschwitz.

"Association took place in this yard," he says. "Prisoners would gather here to socialise, exercise and smoke..."

He exhales the last word like...well, like smoke, and then looks at me before continuing:

"But not ANC members. Mandela instructed all his men to stop smoking as soon as they were interred. That way, he felt, the authorities would have one less means by which to control them."

It's the only part I really listen to, because it's personalised.

Maybe I'll jack the ciggies in. No one controls me except me from now on.

Dan: Poster Boy

At the age of twelve, I was a fairly inactive supporter of animal rights. I joined the Young Ornithologist's Club at school and put an Athena poster of a wounded seal above my bed, its arterial blood seeping into the snow like raspberry sauce on a shaved ice drink. I placed it there deliberately, so the last thing its dying eyes took in would not be my first furtive attempts at masturbation, as I clumsily slid along the nursery slope of my own penis. Instead, it looked out towards an image of the Transformers on the opposing wall, perhaps offering it some vague hope of regenerated life, if only as a wagging tongue in a pair of trapper's boots. Affixed by Blu-Tack, the poster would often fall upon my head as I slept.

Human, clubbed by seal.

Any youthful notions I ever entertained about saving the planet ceased around a year later, the day my own world ended.

They bled from me as I touched my father's headstone for the first time, and it absorbed them all, as terracotta takes in milk.

It was soon after that I realised people are the least protected species of all.

15th March 2016
___

From: danroberts@h–mail.com

To: amonsafari@whizzymail.com.au

___

RE: Seals

Dear Amber,

You were heading into Namibia, eh? With your new-found friends. Did you happen by any chance to visit the seal colony at Cape Cross? Note how I still keep asking you questions – I might as well direct my enquiries toward a pipistrelle bat, or ask a Breville sandwich toaster for its thoughts on economic stimulus packages.

No?

Well, alright then, let me tell you about it. Cape Cross is located on the Skeleton Coast in Namibia, a place as barren and desolate as your cruel Antipodean heart. The seal colony there is one of the more redolent images of Africa that will be forever pan seared upon my retina. Oh, the humanity...

I'll pause for a minute while you look that word up...

...this place was entirely too vivid.

Imagine the opening beach scenes of "Saving Private Ryan" re-shot in fillet-o-fish *Odourama* with an all-pinniped cast and you're somewhere close. Crushed dead pups littering the beach like blubbery draught excluders, forlorn infants bleating away for their mothers lost at sea, bull seals braying and squaring off to each other like gypsies at a wake...then by night the jackals home in like malevolent Wombles to take out all the trash.

Amidst these scenes of devastation, there was one pup that had somehow got itself stuck on the elevated pedestrian boardwalk, stranded from the rest of the group. A German tourist came along and thought he was doing the right thing by liberating it, so he scooped it up in his arms, leaned over the handrail and dropped it back onto the sands.

In his defence, he did it as delicately as the angle would allow, but that does not negate the fact that his actions were equivalent to dumping a new-born baby onto a railway platform from the window of a Pullman carriage. Silly Heinrich's manoeuvre was *nicht gut.* He would have been better employed bludgeoning that unfortunate creature to death with one of his Birkenstocks. The fall completely fucked that pup up, smashed all its guts in. After that, it lay alone on the beach, yelping helplessly and convulsing. Dying.

I watched this hideous vignette unfold but the German was by now oblivious to it. As soon as he'd unwittingly sent the animal hurtling towards a prolonged and painful death, his wife came over and gave him a big sloppy kiss.

Ach, mein hero!

Together they strolled away, arm in arm, towards a blood red sunset. At least there wasn't too much symbolism. He was wearing a pith helmet too. That's why I thought he knew what he was doing. I thought he was the Park Ranger or something when he first rolled up. Who wears a pith helmet of their own volition?

Disgusting story, eh? Another member of the group was with me at the time and actually recorded the entire event on her camera phone. We contemplated leaking it onto YouTube, picturing the blissfully unaware German touching down in Schoenfeld airport to find hordes of irate animal welfare protesters awaiting him:

Babykiller! Babykiller!

Exactly how long would it take to fill a pith helmet with tears, I wonder? But in reality, he probably sleeps the sleep of the just - unaware every night. Whereas we will perhaps be tortured by those images forever. Sometimes they pop into my head when I can't sleep, but when I can't sleep now it's because I'm thinking about you. When I do sleep, I wake up with pins and needles in my arm and proceed to stick them in an effigy of you. So it all gets jumbled up together in my head and then you're the one wearing the pith helmet and I'm the seal. I too am crushed.

You must think me a fool, Amber. For all these weeks, I've been compiling reasons in my head to explain away your lack of response to my emails. After everything you said and all you promised in Cape Town, it never would have even occurred to me that you just don't like me anymore.

No matter what you may think of me, I'm not some imbecile. I didn't just fall off some applecart on the way to The Big Town, with a suckling pig under my arm and straw in my hair. I've been around a bit. I've been almost everywhere but here, mostly anywhere but here. I know all too well how it can go with these holiday romances. It's like Stockholm Syndrome, or when a couple start having it off on Big Brother: fine and dandy as long as it's in that hermetically sealed world, but then you put a little bit of distance between the pair and that's all there is...distance.

You're at the other end of the world, true, but you're still only a mouse-click away. Yet apparently a mouse-click is too Herculean a task for you. Come out of your little hole in the skirting board and explain your inactions at least. Kindly be so gracious as to afford me some sense of closure. I'd say you owe me that much. Rather than leaving me here in limbo like some unbaptized cot death.

Dan.

Amber: Saffer Arseholes

"What do you want to do now?" Dan asks me, on the ferry back from the island.

"We just got out of prison," I say. "Let's go get laid!"

We go for lunch instead, at Victoria waterfront. As I enter the restaurant's terrace, there's a group of fat white South African drunks stuffed into a table, all acting fat and white and South African and drunk. I'm ahead of Dan (who's probably still in the reception area licking a fucking pot-plant or something) and they stop their loud conversation to leer at me. I am frozen to the spot; a rabbit in the headlights at a Monster Truck Arena, until I feel the angel tap of Dan's hand at the small of my back. It's brief, and it's respectful, and it's guiding me past them towards a quiet corner of the plaza.

It's always the corners with this guy. He's like a locker room voyeur.

He orders a steak cut from some animal I've never heard of and I order spaghetti. I like spaghetti; it looks complicated on the plate but it's really simple. I'm just thinking that Dan's more at ease than I've ever seen him (in all my eighteen hours of knowing him) when there's a sudden smashing of crockery and a loud cheer from the Round Table of Round Arseholes. I'm wincing, but Dan practically jumps out of his seat. He obviously hasn't spent as much time around arseholes as I have. I fix them up for a living. And I've been known to take my work home with me.

"How wearisomely predictable," he says looking over at the group, regaining his composure.

People who say things like that should really be wearing red velvet smoking jackets as they do.

"You must hate them," I say.

"South Africans?"

"Drunks," I reply, pushing my glass of wine behind the serviette dispenser discreetly.

"Same thing," he says, smiling. That's better, Danny Boy! Then he ruins it by continuing talking. "Poor is the man whose pleasures depend upon the permission of another."

"Is that Oscar Wilde?" I ask, because I'm still thinking about the smoking jacket and because it's usually always Oscar Wilde.

"It's from a Madonna song," he admits, sheepishly.

"Oh," I say, laughing nervously and wondering if he might be gay. But I think if he were gay he would have a better haircut. "Big fan, are you?"

"No," he says and then looks back towards the men coolly. "I don't hate drunks. The main thing is they *shout*. They shout when they think they're talking. I sit in bars and they shout their opinions and their stories right into my face. When I can't take anymore, when my face is flecked with their saliva, then I retire. Most nights I go to bed early."

"Doesn't sound like such hot shit from your perspective."

"It's still better than the telly," he says, shrugging.

"So, was I like that last night?"

"You weren't whispering," he replies.

The food arrives and we chat as we eat. I am careful to keep my volume at a respectable level. He asks me where I'm from and seems to know Sydney better than I do. Turns out he has some old friend who lives there. We talk about our personal lives. He's English. He's single. No great shocker there; he's probably the most singular person I've ever met. When he asks me about my life, I speak of my ex Neville briefly, giving him the radio-friendly version, edited for violence. But I do mention his mood swings, his obsessive behaviour and his jealousy and only stop when I realise my voice is getting higher and higher and higher and I'm stammering a little and I've over-wound my spaghetti so much it's constricting the handle of my fork.

He's a good listener, but I suppose I've been talking so much I haven't given him any other option. He takes the fork from my hand and gently places it in the pasta bowl, then offers me a napkin for my sauce-splattered hand. I use it to dab away tears instead and look around the room for handily located Fire Exits. At least Dan should know where they are!

"So, what...what...what..." Aw, fuck off with that stammer! I've been doing so well. "What do you think? What do you think about a man like that?"

"Ah, don't do that, Amber," he says.

"Do what?"

"You're a beautiful girl," he says. "You could pose that question to any other heterosexual man and he'll tell you exactly what you want to hear: This bloke was a tosspot. He didn't appreciate you. He was all wrong for you. You could do better. But what he'll really be saying is that he thinks *he's* that better proposition.... and I can't honestly say that about myself."

Jesus.

Dan thinks I am beautiful!

Dan: Twinned With

I've got a job. Sort of. It's almost like a job apart from the bit where they pay you. As part of the government's Get Britain Working scheme, I've been forced into three days a week voluntary work at a local charity shop. Just to keep my hand in, just to keep my runtish snout snuffling at the trough of commerce.

I am being restarted.

I work with two septuagenarian twins called Vi and Esther. They are identical, and as yet I still can't discern between the two. Every time they ask me a question or issue a directive, my response ends with an ungainly pregnant pause as I abort any attempt to hazard a guess as to their moniker.

"No problem, I'll get right on that (/)" I say. Dot dot dot. Your name here.

I consider the fetishistic notions that men attribute to twin sisters and wonder if any rakish charmers, sporting demob suits and brilliantined hair, ever entertained such fantasies about these two. It's hard to imagine now. They look like two bath-crinkled fingers on the same hand. There are great creases in their faces that could capture and safely holster unbroken teardrops. They both sport clip-on earrings attached to globular lobes, as though to stop the flesh from dripping down into their cardigans, dammed by the tissues shoved up their sleeves.

The other day they were discussing an old friend, and one of them offered up this gem:

"You do remember her. We went to line-dancing with her. She always used to wear espadrilles. Anyway, she's got a brain tumour."

Not all of their communication is verbalised. Sometimes, one will laugh at one side of the shop and the other will join in from the backroom. There is never any indication of what they are laughing at. I wonder if they might be slagging me off telepathically. The heightened sense of perception shared by twins makes them a quick study, though. Within ten minutes of my arrival on the first day, they instantly pegged me as some embittered loner with limited social skills, and consigned me to the backroom.

I like it there. I like Vi and Esther and I like the charity shop itself, because I feel comfortable amongst the discarded now. Because I am *so* last season. Everything left on the shelf there has been previously handled, perhaps even dropped. Porcelain dogs regard the clientele through sad, rheumy eyes, looking for a new home, fruitlessly willing their tails to wag. They have been fitted with chips that ensure they won't be returned to their owners.

Neither of the twins ever married or had children. Maybe because they were already two. Presumably, that's why they are now spending their dotage selling battered knick-knacks to mental people and starter home immigrants.

Yesterday, from the backroom, I watched one of the pair, just inches from me but many miles away, tenderly stroking the matted blond hair of a dirt-bruised child's doll. Eventually, her sister came across, planted a wet kiss on her dried cheek, and gently led her over towards the book section by the arm, there to categorise and alphabetise accounts of lives more fruitfully abundant than their own.

It reminded me of something from my past, something I can't bring myself to think about today. Life can be an elbow in the ribs sometimes. Regarding this scene, I felt a tiny sliver of my calcified heart drop into the pit of my stomach and explode like a fallen icicle.

MISSING PERSONS REPORT
NAME: Joy Santos
LAST KNOWN WHEREABOUTS: Dumaguete, Negros,
The Phillipines.
FILED BY: Dan Roberts

Some of the men had been there for so long that they were no longer tanned but stained. By night, when they sat on beanbags in the beach bars, they resembled upended furniture. On the cushions next to them sat their dark pearls, tastefully arranged as though in a jeweller's window.

The men were so old they sometimes had pieces missing. Eyes, legs, lungs, prostates, wives, consciences...Reduced men, men reduced to this. They travelled there to find another piece, to put themselves back together again. Elderly Germans, elderly Russians, English, Dutch, Americans...

The Americans were the easiest to spot. They drank foamy beer and hid their foamy brains from the sun in foamy baseball caps with battleships on the front. They were vets once; just animals now. All they needed was to eat and drink and fuck and find shade.

They sat in silence with their dates. Both parties stunned by circumstance, but in entirely different ways. The girls played with their phones and the men cast their eyes, or their good eye, around the bar. They looked for other men drinking foamy beer and wearing foamy baseball caps with battleships on the front. When they found one, they would chew each other's fat away, reminisce about Shoney's breakfasts and the Green Bay

Packers. Their girls sat next to them, maybe swapped survival tips, compared bloats.

We can only guess what they said to each other:

"My one snores like a pig."

"My one *looks* like a pig."

"Mine sometimes cries when he touches me."

"Which one do you think will die first?"

They giggled then and the men were back In Country.

"Sorry ladies," said one, leant in close, placed a hand on a thigh like invasive surgery. "We were miles away."

The girls nodded and smiled, dutifully and beautifully. Stepford Wives; step-daughters and step-wives combined.

"It's okay," they said, but everyone involved knew that it really wasn't. Then they retired again to their respective corners of the world, all together and still hopelessly alone.

I watched and waited. I told myself I was not like them. But I was in Dumaguete looking for a girl just like they were. Her name was Joy. She was of a petite build, with dark hair and dark eyes. Skin kind of swarthy. A girl like that shouldn't be too hard to locate in The Philippines.

I'd walked around the town all day in the threatening heat, until my arse-crack was a flowing river and my anus its delta. I saw her everywhere and nowhere. On every moped that passed me, eating *balut* at every storefront, hand in hand with every fat white man I swore I was different from.

I had met her two nights previously, saw her dancing in an outdoor nightclub. The strobe light made her look like found footage. She wasn't a prostitute. Prostitutes dance well. It's part of their sales pitch. Joy's awkward moves amongst them made her resemble a doomed salmon. But her scales shone beautifully in the frantic moonlight.

I beckoned her over to my table, which I don't usually do. Even with friends. I had to know her. She wasn't a prostitute any more than any of us are. Most of the girls in The Philippines are prostitutes to some degree. Sometimes they want 2000 pesos upfront. Sometimes they want a visa. Sometimes they want a Jollibee burger. Sometimes they just want you to pay them a compliment.

Joy wanted a frozen margarita. I listened to her talk for hours and the only thing I really remember is that her favourite animals were "butterflies and chickens." After a while, it was like elevator music. I tolerated it because I thought that doing so would take me where I wanted to go. Most *Fillipina's* life stories are seventy years condensed into twenty. They will usually include:

* Teenage pregnancy.
* A feckless, *bolero* ex–boyfriend.
* A raspy need to provide for their child/ren.
* Some death.
* A Western boyfriend who promised them the world, or at least another one. He doesn't call anymore. Just took what he wanted and left.

I was that next Western tourist, waiting to take what I wanted. I felt that if I nodded appreciatively and made my eyes into sinkholes of sorrow periodically I might get it. Not with this one. She was too smart, and still smarting. A mature student then, putting herself through university, studying to be a trainee caregiver, a girl with goals and aspirations. I settled for a dry-lipped peck on the cheek at the end of the night and a promise that we would go out the next day.

I paid her into a private resort with a pool. Used her weightlessness in the water to impress her with my strength. Rubbed her shoulders and bought her a fruit smoothie. At the end of the day, she dropped me back at my hotel on her moped and kissed me with a wet and chlorinated mouth, a kiss that would linger like a communion wafer; a kiss I can still taste. I arranged to meet her in a nearby bar at 8pm.

I waited until 11.30, watching the Americans and their girls. The silence of the watch I never wear became deafening, the hand of a metronome repeatedly tapping against my forehead. She didn't show up. Dumaguete is a small city, but I never saw or heard from her again after that. For the next few days, I could sense her outrunning me at every corner, the exhaust fumes from her disappearing scooter a raspberry blowing directly in my foolish, trusting face.

She wasn't anywhere I could find her, but I do hope she's somewhere with somebody now. I hope she's graduated and found work. I hope she's pushing back the nicotined cuticles of an elderly Oregonian, caring for him so he'll keep her bastard child in breakfast cereal. I hope he playfully slaps her behind when she's finished, then drinks a beer and fans himself with a foamy baseball cap with a battleship on the front. I hope she looks down at her own hands sometimes, life-hardened already, and thinks about just what she let slip through them.

She wasn't a prostitute. If she was, she would have turned up. All I ever wanted from her was her attention. She couldn't even give me that.

Dan: Aria 51

The best part of working at the charity shop is that I get first dibs on the incoming stock. On my very first shift, I came across something quite special. A beautifully tailored, Merino wool, pinstriped Ozwald Boateng suit. Sometimes the graders in the warehouse these items are dispatched from aren't always aware of the value of the goods they are handling. This was evidenced by the fact that the suit was already marked up at £5, whereas the drab Burtons suit folded beneath it was priced at £7.50. When I spy a bargain like this, my first response is always to look around for the hidden camera.

I took it to one of the twins at the counter and actually blushed as I paid for it. It made me feel bad that I am perhaps profiting from the oversights of the elderly, kind-hearted volunteers who forgo their Channel 5 afternoon movies to help the poor and needy expand their wardrobes. I tried to console myself with the knowledge that maybe at least some Eritreans got a couple of new buckets out of the transaction. Perhaps, on their eight-mile daily walk to the nearest well, passers-by will whistle appreciatively, and their once concave chests will suddenly expand with pride.

When I got home I couldn't resist trying the suit on. It fitted perfectly, but I struggled in vain to think of when I would have occasion to wear it. Another court appearance, perhaps?

It suddenly struck me that the first time I would wear this suit would undoubtedly be at my Grandma's funeral.

I couldn't have that. It felt like I was orchestrating her demise just by buying it. So, on Saturday, I took the money I was saving for my flight to Australia and attended an opera for the very first time.

I still had some money left over, so my date for the evening was a Slovenian prostitute named Ilke. I found her on a website for Sheffield-based escorts. I chose her because she had a happy, pixellated face and listed her number two favourite pastime as going to the opera. Number one was "walking at the moon." I chose her because she looked nothing like Amber.

I met her outside the Civic Theatre. Her face looked a lot happier when it was pixellated. She was dressed more for a night at the dog track than the opera. The £10 ticket, the one where you get a free Tote bet and a chicken burger. With her pallid white flesh spilling over the top of a low cut black dress she looked like a pint of Guinness poured by a lunatic.

"Are you Dafe?" she enquired.

For a second I thought she was asking if I was deaf. But then that didn't make sense, because she was enquiring in such a low voice.

"No, I'm not Dave. I'm Dan," I said.

"Dafe, Dan. We are married? No difference to me. You haf money?"

I handed it over and that was the first and last time she smiled that evening, a revolving bow tie pinned onto an Easter Island statue.

"Nice suit," she said, as we entered the building.

It was worth it just for that moment, though.

I always thought the opera was one of those things that people pretended to like, like sushi, or the French. I wanted to see one just to say I'd done it, and I didn't really expect to enjoy it. But it's a thrilling experience. I can't even remember what this one was called now, and I had no idea what was going on, but it didn't really seem to matter. It featured sex, intrigue, and betrayal. It was quite the night away from my troubles.

I think it helped that we were sat in the second row, right by the orchestra. The bloke on the kettledrums was right in front of me. Every time some woman on stage started warbling a bit, I'd see him prepping himself and that was always the tip-off. He'd take a little swig of water, crack his knuckles, and then BOOM BOOM BOOM BOOM he'd be off. Then the rest of the orchestra would start chiming in, and before you knew it some seemingly steady little aria had got ideas above its station and built itself up to a big deafening climax, that makes all the hairs on your arm feel like they're scurrying towards your shoulders, like Goths to Whitby.

Back at the Premier Inn, Ilke had disrobed before I even figured out how to work the dimmer switch. She lay naked and motionless on top of the sheets. She was a big unit when prised out of her figure-hugging dress, obviously none too bashful about ladling a couple of dumplings in with her serving of goulash, or whatever it is that Slovenians eat. The wan and goose-pimpled flesh around her meaty thighs made her look like a turkey waiting to be basted.

A real woman though, not some principal boy type like the Australian. I eased in next to her and watched her watching the ceiling for a while before moving closer. Disturbingly, I was reminded of my Grandma, staring at the artexed wall in the nursing home. I wondered what she was thinking. I didn't doubt for a second that she had seen things in her life that I could not even begin to contemplate. Probably even within the last week.

But I wasn't going to be one of those men who asked if we could just talk. I moved closer.

"You haf woman legs," she said.

"Thanks."

"No kiss," she said, angling her face away from mine.

No kiss, no loss. Women's lies are communicable through their saliva. I ran a clammy hand down over her wide frame.

"No touch inside," she said.

It felt like a Health and Safety course. There didn't seem to be much else I was allowed to do except fuck her, so I gave up and did that. BOOM BOOM BOOM BOOM. I fantasised that I was the one client who actually gave her pleasure, the one person who did touch her inside. But I don't think she even knew I was there. Her die-cast face betrayed no feelings other than tolerance. A pixellated mind.

Once in a while, Ilke would mutter the odd nugget of encouragement, but the words were spoken in a tranced-out monotone, as though she were dictating a shopping list to a slow child. I ground away at her, furiously and joylessly. I could have got the same effect with a blow-up doll and I wouldn't have had to buy it an opera ticket either.

Now even women I pay recoil from me. Thrown off my game by her nonchalance, I gave up halfway through. I apologised on behalf of myself and every man who'd been near her. Not that any of us ever got close. I tipped her an extra £20 as a thank you for managing to conceal her disgust, a feat that I couldn't manage.

No wonder they call it tricking.

"Good night, Dafe," she said, already out the door, already mentally licking the stamp that would send the money home to buy pistons for the tractor and that first pair of buckle-up shoes for her child.

After she was gone, I finished myself off in the bathroom. I thought about Amber, imagined taking her on the sink, her head smashing back against the mirror as I came.

Crescendo. Shower curtain fall.

I stayed in the shower for the longest time, struggling to find the perforation for the sachet of shampoo provided, eventually giving up. I tossed it towards the hirsute plughole, and watched it flapping against the force of the water, a dying tilapia fish that never made it to the delta. As for the condom, the offending and defending article that travelled into Slovenia and back, that remained where I sloughed it. Going unnoticed in the sink, until I spat my travel-sized Colgate upon its palsied form like a liniment in the morning.

Dan: Requiem for a Saveloy

Other than the traditional indulgences of the opera and a Slovenian prostitute, my birthday went as unmarked as a leper's grave. No card from Amber, except for the obvious red card. One came through from my mother, as it occasionally does. Every couple of years she remembers who I am.

Thinking of you, it said. The other 353 days she thinks only of herself and the off-licence's closing time.

Postmark local, her forever distant.

She was even absent from the last birthday of mine she had been present at. With odd symmetry, I turned thirteen six-and-half weeks after my father's death. A few evenings prior to that, she'd crashed into my room and knelt next to me as I lay reading. She'd steadied herself on the bedside cabinet and leaned in close, too close. I could taste her odour in my mouth; orchard-scrumped apples decaying in a Co-op bag. I knew she'd been drinking because she was looking at me. She couldn't do that back then without soaking her eyes in alcohol first.

"I know it won't be the same without…"

I glared down at my comic book; wished I could slide behind the panels and hide from her.

"But it is still your birthday," she went on, regardless. "We should do something."

When I said nothing she ruffled my hair, the first time she'd touched me in weeks. I caved in beneath her cold fingers, opened myself to negotiations. It was agreed that a party was unsuitable, being as the last group of people in our house had buried the homeowner. I was to invite my best mate Tommy around for a special tea.

"It'll be nice," she said, standing up too quickly after a botched and faithless forehead kiss. "I'll bake a cake. Things will be better."

I wanted to believe her. I think I almost might have done if she hadn't spent five minutes trying to locate the light switch on the way out, even though I was reading by lamp glare.

On the day, Tommy and I walked back from school together. My coccyx was still pinging like sonar from the bumps I'd received on the games field at last break. He was more excited than I was. I'd been to one of his parties a few years before. I remembered being scared by the unexplained dried blood in the bathroom sink and an embarrassment that swept through the small flat like an airborne virus when the present I gave him turned out to be more expensive than those from his family. He didn't have any birthday parties after that.

As soon as we went around the back of my house, we could see the smoke pouring out of the open kitchen door.

I've lost another one, was my first thought.

I rushed inside and dimly made out the centrepiece of the set table through the haze. It might have been a cake once, briefly. I have thought of its appearance only once before now: when I watched dried yak dung burn on a fire somewhere in the frigid heart of the Mongolian steppe.

Regarding it then, I was glad I'd been at school and thus unable to lick the mixing bowl like I usually do. My Grandma was standing over the torched abortion, fanning at it frantically with a tea towel. She was still strong then. She would have been better served drop-kicking it down the garden, but she might have broken a toe.

I've never known how she came to be there, there was no way my mother would have invited her. But she only lived four streets away from us, so maybe she saw the smoke signals.

"Boys!" she cried, startled by our appearance, ushering us out into the backyard like ducklings. "There's been a...well...things are...*buggered* really."

"Where's Mrs Roberts?" Tommy asked. It had to come from him. I'd stopped looking for her weeks ago. He was still surveying the carnage of the kitchen. Tommy was a big fan of food. It hit him hard, although I now wonder if he thought the thing on the table may have been my mother's head.

"She's...erm...she's having a little lie down. She's very tired today."

Tommy and I exchanged glances. We were both thirteen then, not twelve. We knew what that was code for.

My Grandma disappeared back into the smoke and emerged moments later, delving into her purse and spluttering.

"Here's a couple of quid, Danny," she said. "You two lads go and get yourselves something from the chippy while I tidy up and have a talk with your Mam. Don't rush back. Have a walk around and get some fresh air. You can both come to mine for your tea tomorrow, if you like."

I nodded like the dulled child I was becoming and moved away from the smouldering house, taking my bewildered best friend with me.

"Happy birthday, love," my Grandma called to the closing gate.

We sat on our school jumpers on a damp bench by the fishing ponds and ate our meal in silence until Tommy spoke up.

"They all do it," he said, wiping greasy fingers on his parka. "My Mam drinks too. She waits 'til I've gone to bed. I've seen her. When I go for a piss."

"Except mine stops drinking *when* I go to bed," I replied, taking a perfectly good battered sausage and throwing it into the water. To hurt Tommy for trying to help me. To watch it sink.

Amber: Fucked

Too much overcooked pasta and raw emotion. I feel bloated and empty. Too much wine. Too much whining. Too much sun and not enough night before it.

"I'm shattered," I announce to Dan in the restaurant as we settle the bill. I go Dutch with my Englishman, a straight 50/50, so thankfully I'm spared all that usual budget backpacker bullshit about who had the bread rolls and who didn't. Although, he did order the steak. Maybe he's a bludger, a modest extortionist, who plans to bleed me dry a dollar at a time. Maybe I'll never trust a man again. Maybe I'll never trust myself to choose a man again.

"Do you want to go home?" he asks.

"I just got here!"

"I meant back to the hostel."

Duh, Amber.

"Ah. I think maybe I have to. Crashing and burning a bit now."

"Want me to come with you?"

"Bit forward, isn't it?"

"I meant that...that I'd see you back safely," he says, a little flustered. That's cute as. Bless his little cotton sockies. Someone's stammering and for once, it isn't me. I had him on the ropes for a second there, but he'll return to his precious corner before I can swing another haymaker.

"I reckon maybe I'll just get a taxi. You're welcome to jump in with me, though."

She added hopefully.

"Thought I might look around for a bit longer," he says. "Apparently there's a submarine here somewhere."

A submarine. Whoop-de-fucking-doo. Boys and their bath toys. Girls play with conditioners and body scrubs instead. Try to make themselves beautiful to attract mongrels who'd rather be chasing cars. Or submarines.

Here's the awkward sign-off! Do I go for a hug, a kiss, a boot up the arse, or what? He offers me his hand instead, warm and damp like a dog's nose. Cheers, mate. Poms are just Australians with manners. I tell him I'll see him later and head back to the hostel, sensing his absence on the big hot leatherette backseat of the taxi, and in the gurning face of its driver who thoughtfully rearranges his rear view mirror so he can speak directly to my breasts.

Thankfully, everyone else is out when I get back to the dorm. I have another little strategic cry – don't even know what it's about, really, just cleaning the pipes out – then fall heavy on my bed.

When I wake up, it's dark again. But I feel lighter.

1st April 2016

From: danroberts@h–mail.com

To: amonsafari@whizzymail.com.au

RE: Age

Dear Amber,

Was it the age difference? Feel free to not answer honestly. Seven years is quite a lot, I suppose. For me, it was quite a result to be squiring some twenty-six-year-old girl around Cape Town, but perhaps from your perspective it wasn't such a square deal. You did say that it was irrelevant to you, but now it appears *I'm* irrelevant to you, so possibly it crossed your mind.

I really don't know any more. I'm just clutching at cheese straws now, in a buffet of bewilderment. Maybe you espied an unsightly nostril hair of mine glinting in the South African sun and started running mental calculations on how long it would be before this affliction spread to my ears. Every time I pull one of those hairs out, I automatically hold it up to the light to inspect its dimensions. Had I a camera to hand, I would pose with my catch like a proud fisherman.

Or, perhaps you started thinking about how when I was forty you'd be thirty-three, my age now. I know they say forty's the new thirty, but then that would make thirty the new twenty. There's no way you could ever catch me up, no scope to meet in the middle.

Forty's the new thirty.

You're only as old as you feel.

Age is just a number.

I've always steadfastly tried to avoid these adages because it's only really old people who need to use them, to justify the fact that they're still around consuming vital resources of oxygen. Contrary to popular opinion, it is old people, not cats, who steal kid's breath. And now I am old, I suppose, at least comparatively.

Remember how when you were a kid at Christmas you were always disappointed when one of the gifts you received from your parents was underwear? Because parents are contractually obligated to buy your socks and underpants all year round, it's a waste of a present.

But now when I think of Christmas coming around, I look forward to it because I could always use new socks. I'm guessing that the realisation of that is the demarcation point, the Checkpoint Charlie leading into curmudgeonliness. That's when you know that you're old, you might as well just accept it and focus on the business at hand: buying bags of broken biscuits from market stalls and poring over seed catalogues.

I had to go for a medical check-up before the Africa trip and the nurse attending asked me if I'd had any health problems.

"Just the odd bit of lower back pain," I said. "And, occasionally, a recurring groin strain...a bit of muscular stiffness, and my chest sometimes gets tight in the night."

"Nothing to worry about," she said, even her voice sounding like a latex glove being snapped off a hand. "You'll find that once you're past the age of thirty, the body will start to deteriorate fairly rapidly."

Thanks for that.

Thirty-two years old, and already beginning the inexorable slide towards death. Bits and pieces of me crumbling and falling away like a Tibetan sand mandala. It only seems like five minutes ago that I was putting lollipop sticks in the spokes of my BMX.

I can't say that I'm hung up about my age, but if I had the chance I'd much rather be younger. Because I'd have more time. I suppose all this travelling malarkey is really just some subconscious ploy to outrun death. Or maybe my mother. I always need to be pushing forward to new frontiers, never the same place twice. I believe that everything we see and do in some way informs who we are, so we should try to see as much as we can. Through travel, I'm compiling a show-reel of sights and sounds and storing them all in a dusty annexe of my brain. Come the day of reckoning, as my life ebbs from me on a plastic-sheeted bed in some taupe room, all these images will hopefully flicker through the zoetrope of my atrophying mind.

And I want it to be cinematic.

Your warm smile is the one thing from all my travels that I ever felt the need to see again immediately. And now you can't even write back. A group of monkeys locked together in a room with word processors would have probably given up on Shakespeare by now and cobbled together an email to me. So, what's your excuse?

I'm not so bad, am I?

Dan.

Dan: Monkeys and Magpies

I read an article about monkeys the other day. It was on the internet, so it must be true. The piece in question concerned an incident that happened in Bangladesh a few years ago. Or was it Bangalore? Maybe it was even Bangor; an Englishman can never truly know what kind of mischief is afoot in Wales, it's like the United Kingdom's own Area 51. The Dai is fast, as soon as they smell us approaching they shoo all the dragons away to hide behind a veil of malice.

The only reason Wales seems to exist at all is to provide scale: newsreaders always say that the area of rainforest depleted was the size of Wales, or that a military faction were caught with enough explosive devices to wipe out all of Wales. It's hard to care too much when they use analogies like that.

But I think maybe it was Bangalore. Anyway, it was some place where monkeys roam freely amongst the local populace. The market traders constantly have to fend off these thieving primates. In this instance, a monkey tried to steal a mango and the grocer went for it with a scimitar. He didn't score a full contact blow but he managed to lop the creature's tail off. As it lay there bleeding to death in the street, a horde of other simians descended from the rooftops. In a bizarre imitation of the human behaviour they witness every day, they then picked up their fallen comrade and carried him into the police station.

This is the problem with monkeys. I like watching them on the telly when they're in their natural surroundings – drinking mugs of tea and blithely roller-skating around with their natty little waistcoats on – but when they cross over into the human world: problems. Consumerist society destroys their value systems and before you know it, they're ripping a woman's face off.

Everyone always bangs on about how apes are the closest thing to man, about how gorillas have a 93.9% match with human DNA. It all seems very impressive until you look into it a bit further and you see that even something like a stoat runs at about 74%.

Monkeys look to humans to see how to act in the same way that children do. After the death of my father and the subsequent sinking of my mother, I spent my formative teenage years being shuttlecocked from one foster home to the next. Permanently lost, perennially looking for tutelage and guidance from a selection of poorly cast role models.

The best placement I had was the summer I spent on a farm situated on the outskirts of my hometown. The farmer who took me in looked like a mournful-eyed lurcher that had been trained to walk upright in a pair of wellington boots, all wiry, whiskery and greyed. His wife seemed as though she had been strained through the same cloth, but with a burst-capillary glow to her cheeks, and messy blonde hair that straw would get lost in.

They weren't like most of the others. They were good people, reserved, but kind. They welcomed me into their childless and modest little house, but never tried to be my parents. I was a mere twenty minute walk from my own home, but far enough away for it to feel like I was on another planet.

Farm kids are expected to work for their keep in the same way that ratting farm cats are. Again, this suited me, and I threw myself headlong into the jobs at hand, grateful for something to take my mind away from dark thoughts of my former life. Most evenings I would go to bed mercifully too tired to dream.

One swelteringly hot day the farmer and I were in the front field uprooting the poisonous ragwort that had bloomed there, before the horses could eat it. The best part of the working day was always when lunchtime came around. He would give me a pound and send me over to the Farm Shop next door to bring back a jug full of goat's milk. I would run over there and then walk slowly back, holding the big, heavy jug before me like a trophy as I carefully negotiated the uneven land.

On this day, after I returned, we sat on the shaded side of the tractor, resting our aching backs against the big wheel of the trailer we had been loading. We hungrily devoured our foil-wrapped sandwiches and took turns drinking from the big jug. The old woman in the Farm Shop always kept the milk well chilled, and as you drank it, you could feel the little shards of ice cracking and dissolving in your mouth. It was like swallowing nutritious glass. Raising the jug, I spilled some down my T-shirt and the farmer wiped it away with a none-too-clean looking hankie.

"Done well today, lad," he said, smiling and squeezing my shoulder. A wiry grip, a Claymation figure with a pipe cleaner skeleton. For once, I didn't flinch.

I smiled back awkwardly and blushed. As far as the taciturn farmer went, this was a superlative. I spent the rest of the afternoon pulling weeds out of the ground at twice my previous speed, keen to reclaim his approval. I began to fantasise about a new life as laird to the estate. I imagined a birthday where the farmer would present me with a waxed jacket just like his, while his wife plucked a chicken over her blanketed knee and looked on approvingly, her cheeks glowing in the way that only country folks' do.

It didn't quite work out.

Sundays were a half-day. After chores in the morning followed by lunch, the farmer and I would walk down the land together, while his wife curled up on the couch to watch the *Eastenders* omnibus. We would look in on the livestock briefly, or pause to inspect an ear of corn, but mostly we just walked along in an amenable silence, shattered only by the occasional report of his shotgun as he took the pot-shots at passing game birds.

One Sunday, the farmer stopped and pointed across the field.

"See there," he said. "Maggies' nest."

Farmers despise magpies because they steal life. They take eggs and chicks, and have even been known to peck the eyes from new-born lambs. They have a pathological hatred of them, one as pure as goat's milk, one that spills over and blanches out all their other sensibilities. I squinted vaguely in the direction of the tree-line, unsure where I was supposed to be looking. The first I saw of the nest was it plummeting, after the deafening boom of the farmer's 12-bore. Then we began walking over towards it.

The fallen nest had survived the peppering blast almost intact, save two clumps of twigs that were sticking up from it like hands raised in surrender. The six chicks inside the nest were all still alive, loudly chirping. The farmer gave the fragile domicile a single, tokenistic kick and then ground one of the young to pieces under his riding boot.

"Get on, ya bad sod," he muttered, his face now a warped, clearance sale Halloween mask. Then he stepped on another one.

"Will you try it?" he asked, then looking to me.

I stood as the beech tree before me, rooted to the ground, swaying in the wind. I looked at the farmer, his shotgun now broken over the crook of his arm, barrels resting in a crease of his waxed jacket. His pale blue eyes searched me out, expectantly. I stepped towards the nest and closed my eyes. Lifted my leg and brought it crashing down. Felt twigs cracking under the sole of my foot.

"You missed," he said.

I whitened as I looked back down at the nest. Four chicks still remained, all featherless and blind, yet seemingly looking right up at me through raw, membranous eyelids. Expectantly, as though I were their mother.

Mother. There's an image I could work with.

My foot came down again, more forcefully and better aimed this time. I felt a tiny skull popping under it, like that hideous, morning-sullying feeling you get when you step on a snail. The worst was the noise, like a wishbone snapping, still back-dropped by that constant chirping. Tiny little noises that deafened me. At that, I thought of biology lessons, of the small bone inside the human ear, also shaped like a wishbone.

To drown it all out I began shouting wildly, hurling nonsensical obscenities down at the nest. "You bastards! You dirty little fuck-bastards! Shitpigs, I'll fucking kill you, you bad little sods!"

All the while, my foot was slamming down and down into the nest like a jackhammer. When I finally stopped, everything in it was obliterated.

Shaking, I wiped a trail of saliva from my chin and looked up at the farmer. In trying to gain his approval, I had garnered only his revulsion. A man who spent his every day corralling animals now looked at me as though I were something he'd stepped in. He turned abruptly and began walking back down the land.

"Tha' were onny supposed to kill 'em," he said, over his shoulder. "Tha' weren't supposed to like it."

I stood there alone in the field for what seemed like the longest time, with all my failings smeared across the sole of my Monkey boot. Out there in the open, amidst so much life and stood right next to its opposite number.

On my very first night in the farmhouse, I woke up in the middle of the night needing to pee. Heading for the toilet, I accidentally walked into the wrong room. It was a nursery. The small draught caused by my opening the door caused the Winnie The Pooh mobile above the cot to give a slight turn and emit a single chime. The room was spotlessly clean and untouched, the only less than pristine thing in it was the painting on the far wall. The tiny handprints of a child, rendered in bright fabric paint. A single, thin trickle of red paint ran down the paper and ebbed into the name pencilled at the bottom:

Aiden, aged 18 months.

The farmer's son, a stolen life. The coloured painting on the wall both the beginning and the end of a cruelly stunted growth chart.

When the top of the farmer's head had finally receded from view I slowly followed his trail back down the balk.

After that incident, he hardly ever looked at me at all. Come the end of the summer, when all the hay was baled, I had served my purpose and was returned to the system. Order something from the seconds catalogue and you shouldn't be too surprised if it turns up chipped. Most of these foster parents would accept me into their home as though I were a new puppy, and then send me right back to the rescue home when I started chewing up the breakfast bar.

Monkey see, monkey don't. Monkeys would do well to look anywhere other than at man for lessons in how to live. They should direct their attentions to the columns of ants marching up their trees in perfect synchronicity, and seek to ape their behaviour. They would be better served considering the mores of the mites they pick from each other's scalps.

Anything's better than us.

Dan: The Coventry Dilemma

"Do you need anything?" I asked. "Is there anything I can bring you?"

I was seated beside her bed. She said nothing, just looked at me like I'd betrayed her. Like it was me that had put her there. But it *was* me that had put her there. Then she rolled onto her back and stared at the ceiling. Her brow furrowed in concentration. She was wishing someone away, I don't know if it was me or herself. I sat in silence with and without her, interrupted only when a drop of her urine trickled through one of the fissures of her rubberized sheets and splashed onto my shoe.

Her message was clear, fluid and fluent: I would rather lie here in my own piss than speak to you.

It's nothing personal. She isn't talking to anyone; the nurses say she hasn't spoken for over a week. She's old and tired, and she just doesn't want to play anymore. She will display no further tolerance of the ridiculous, fleshy puppets that dance before her. She has no more time for us.

I pushed the buzzer by the bed and looked around the room as I waited. Someone had brought her flowers again. Who keeps bringing her those flowers? Perhaps her old friend Bert, from around the corner. I myself brought fruit, knowing full well that it would rot away in a bowl right next to her bed, petals from the wilting flowers falling amidst the peaches. My Grandma rejects these symbols of life now, because she has resigned herself to the alternative. Yet the alternative is a word I can't even bring myself to type in relation to my father's mother.

11th April 2016

From: danroberts@h–mail.com

To: amonsafari@whizzymail.com.au

RE: Monk

Dear Amber,

Round this neck of the woods, if someone's giving us the silent treatment we say they've "got the monk on". In fact, we say they've "got monk on" – because we don't acknowledge the existence of the word "the" in our Yorkshire diction; we replace it with a barely perceptible glottal stop, a slightly Zulu-esque tongue click that can also be used to open automated garage doors.

Actually, that's quite an antiquated expression now. It's more likely that we'd just describe said person as a "mardy bastard". Let me put that in a randomly generated sentence to help you out: "Amber is a mardy bastard." But thematically that wouldn't be a very good fit for this email, so let's now return to the matter of today's presentation: Monks.

Perhaps one day your travels will take you to Tibet. You should try to go before the Chinese eat it, swallow it up like they did the Panchen Lama, because it's a very special place. I'm just some Northern monkey from a pokey little pit town, I can hardly credit some of the places I've managed to make it to. Before I went, I never even thought of Tibet as a real place. It sounds like some mythical kingdom.

Anyway, if you do make it there you should check out Sera Monastery, home of the debating monks. I know that doesn't sound too exciting, but trust me on this one, Amber, it really is quite the show. Picture a beautiful, sun-dappled courtyard full of Tibetan monks in their deep red robes. After a bit of preliminary chanting they split off into twos. In these pairings, one monk sits cross-legged on the floor while the other one stands over him, giving him a load of slaver about whatever the topic may be. Obviously, I didn't know what they were debating – Coke versus Pepsi maybe, the price of yak's butter – but you wouldn't imagine that a chance encounter of Buddhists (to give them their proper collective noun) could get so rowdy. They start wagging their fingers at each other and swinging their prayer beads around like 50's B-movie hoodlums with bike chains. Then, when they've made a particularly salient point, they do this little hand clap thing right under the other monk's nose:

In your face, Brother Gyatso! Use a prayer flag as a napkin – you got served!

Actually, even now that I've described it, it still doesn't sound that good – but again, trust me, you really have to be there. And this is Buddhism we're speaking of, so even if you're not there you're probably where you're meant to be, it's all alright. It was one of the best things I've ever seen, like a Drama Club full of sentient beings re-enacting an episode of Jerry Springer.

I say it *was* one of the best things I've ever seen, because after that I read a book about Tibet. Turns out that because so many monks have become disenfranchised with Chinese involvement in Tibet a lot of them have disrobed in disgust. Or played Follow the Leader and gone off to join the Dalai Lama Version 14.0 in Dharamasala. His new place up in the hills of McLeod Ganj isn't a patch on Potala Palace but, as ever, it's really all about location, location, location. Hence, many of these monks at Sera Monastery are in fact actors; Disneyworld parade Mickeys and Goofys, stooges employed by the Chinese to offer up some bowdlerized version of Tibetan culture to gullible, snap-happy tourists like me.

Regarding Sera Monastery, I perhaps should have been tipped off when I spotted one of the felonious monks text-messaging during incantations. Naively, I assumed he was Googling some theological issue on his Blackberry. The overall experience left me feeling foolish and cheated, and now I'm experiencing similar feelings about you.

You were so adamant about how you wanted me to come over to Sydney as soon as you were back at home; you said that was all you wanted. Once more, I've been duped. You're a flim-flam man, a snake-oil vendor, a flippertygibbet, and you change your tune quicker than an iPod shuffle. In fact, you're not even playing any tune – it's just unacceptable levels of graphic silence with you. Maybe *you are* a Buddhist; that would at least go some way to explaining your level of inaction.

You promise tiramisu and then don't even serve toast.

Dan.

Amber: Peter Dieter Bratwurst Eater

I kipped all the afternoon away and now it's seven in the evening. I hope to Christ it rained on everyone who stayed awake, that always makes me feel better about my time wastage. If I want to get back into the right sleep pattern, it seems like I'm going to have to take a drink now, although I really glean no pleasure from it...Your Honour.

I wonder if I could get a cider, that's sort of like breakfast alcohol. Ah, no: a nicely chilled glass of Savlon would be lovely. I know that it's called Sauvignon now, but I still call it Savlon. That cow Lozzer knew all along, used to giggle behind her cocktail menu when I tried to order it in bars.

Communal showers – yuck. All the hairs in the plughole might be from residents of six different countries. Someone's probably been sick in here within the last week. Someone's probably *had sex* in here within the last week, dirty dogs. Ooh, someone's left some quality shampoo in here, though! I'm nabbing that, as compo for all I'm being made to endure.

I doll myself up a bit, because you never know who's looking. Not too tarty, though, because I think Da...I think whoever I may bump into tonight mightn't like that.

I enter the bar. It's always an anxious moment, as everyone looks round and gives you the once-over. They should serve drinks just outside the bar to help you get your nerve up. But then I suppose people would gather there and stare instead.

He's on me in an instant, before I even make it to the actual bar. He gets me trapped against a pillar like a tethered goat, his arm blocking my way.

"Amber," he says; then gawps at me as I wait for him to say something else. He's drunk already, his breath reeks of beer and barbeque. It's just like being at home.

"I was...I was heading to the bar, Peter," I say.

"Let me come with you."

"I can find it on my own, thanks," I reply.

It's right behind your big bovine shoulder if you'd just move out of the fucking way. I'm up on tippy-toes glancing past him, looking for Dan. He's not in his usual spot at the end of the bar, the bastard. Peter's face is looming in at mine again. I recoil backwards as though I'm warming up for a limbo dance.

"We should talk about this thing between us, Amber," he says.

I'm such a dummy. I actually look at the rapidly decreasing space in the middle of our two bodies.

"There is...nothing between us, Peter," I say. "Just a foot of stale air and your semi-erect penis."

He glances down at his cargo shorts and I use the moment to knock his arm from the pillar, spinning him round ninety degrees. Then I slide right past him like a feminist ninja.

"Dieter," I hear him croak forlornly at my back. "My name is Dieter."

Whatever. I practically run to the bar. I order two glasses of wine. One's from me and one's a gift from the Old Me, who insists on buying the New Me a drink. Seems rude to refuse. I down the first one while the second's still breathing and I'm not. When the warmth rises up in me I finally exhale, then turn and lean my elbows back on the bar. I'm trying for cocky, but probably just look like a King's Cross prozzie.

And there's Dan. He's sat all on his lonesome in a little booth, smiling up at me wryly. I've no idea where he's staying in this hostel, but he seems to have the ability to teleport through it at will. There's a little notebook and a pen on the table.

"Thirsty, Amber?"

He pushes out a stool with his foot. What a true gent he is.

"You keeping a travel journal?" I ask, sitting down, wondering if I'm in it.

"Something like that," he replies, hurriedly pocketing the notebook, flushing slightly. "I like to write stuff down. It helps me to make sense of things."

I ought to start doing that. The last thing I remember writing was a shopping list on the back of a hospital payslip. It's still stuck to my fridge with saliva. It looks like this:

Must buy:
Post-Its

"Did you find your precious submarine?" I ask, trying to change the subject, sparing him.

"No," he replies, laughing, seeming relieved. "That's the thing about submarines. They can be tricky to locate. Especially when you look for them in large bodies of water."

"I suppose so," I say, nervously sweeping my own periscope around, looking for the German. Das Cunt.

"Everything okay?"

"Yeah. No. Dunno."

"You seem pretty certain about that."

I take a big glug from the second glass and set it down.

"I could...I could do with you not being a smartarse for five minutes, Dan, if you can manage that, please."

"Your hands are shaking," he says, very serious now. "Tell me what's wrong."

"It's just, just this guy..."

I see him hold his breath in then. Is that a small flicker of jealousy, maybe? Wooh. I can't say it's my favourite emotion, but a little bit of green looks good on Dan.

"He's kind of stalking me through the hostel, keeps trying to crack onto me," I continue.

"Do you want me to talk to him?"

I love how he offers to do that straight away, without even knowing what the other guy's built like. My hero.

"Nah," I say, taking another pelt on the wine, relaxing a little now. "He'll be alright. Can I just stay here with you, though?"

He leans forward across the table and places his hands gently on my shoulders. I'm suddenly glad I epilated thoroughly before the trip.

"You're a strong and confident woman, Amber..." he begins.

"No, I'm not," I protest.

"You are. You came all the way to Africa on your own."

"I'm joining a tour group, Dan."

"You...fucking hell, let me finish, would you?"

"Okay," I say, laughing.

"You're a strong and confident woman, Amber," he says. Take Two! "You don't need to hide behind any man's coat-tails. If this bloke's bothering you, you ask him politely to stop. If he persists, you tell him to stop more forcefully. If he carries on beyond that, you smack the fucker! Or point him in my direction. I'll offer him some tutelage."

Dan keeps doing this, eh? He gives you the bare conversational minimum all day and then...wallop! It's an odd little speech, but I swear if he weren't holding me up, I might swoon. I like his hands on me. The last time a man put his hands on my shoulders it was to prove how weak I was, but that man knows different now. So I am strong. I'm a hundred fucking feet tall, dangerous and slightly drunk. Consider yourself warned, world!

"I understand what you're telling me," I say. "But...but I really want to stay here with you, Dan."

"Oh," he replies. "Well, then, okay."

He smiles and scooches over in the squeaky little booth. I step around the table to sit next to him. He doesn't say anything then, and I'm learning that's when he tells me the most. From our own tiny world there, we look out upon the one that everyone else lives in.

I'm in his corner now. And he's in mine.

Dan: Death and Venice

Venice is full of murderers. All who visit the city are instrumental in its demise, their footsteps tamping it down into the sea forever. Future generations may well speak of it the way we now mention Atlantis.

There, I sat at an outdoor cafe in Plaza San Marco and absolved my complicity in the shadow of its church. As my cooling coffee swallowed up a biscotti, I viewed the mobilized identity parade of suspects callously stamping the square to death.

One of my duties in the charity shop is Quality Control. Its sounds officious, but what it mostly means is that I sit in the backroom and count out jigsaw pieces. Today, the puzzle under scrutiny was an oil paint depiction of the aforementioned plaza. All too predictably, there was one piece missing.

For a moment, I couldn't help but wonder if I might be in it.

The bell on the shop's door tolled, a Fisher Price facsimile of San Marco's tower. I heard a familiar voice speaking to one of the twins, felt it as an ice-pick in my spine. Innocent sounding, but guilty as hell.

"I've been having a bit of a clear out," she said. "Thought you might want these."

It was my mother. She'd crawled out from under a rock and dragged a bin bag full of her lichen bedding with her. If I'd just leant over a couple of inches I would have been able to see around the dividing wall, see her face for the first time in years. I chose to go the other way instead, slipped out of my chair and gently eased the fire escape door open.

I entered the narrow rear alleyway and crouched behind the skip, head in my hands. I calculated how long the exchange inside the shop would take and then counted in my head. One elephant, two elephant, three elephant...visualised them all crossing the savannah with trunks wrapped around tails, forming a daisy-chain for the Gods. I went all the way up to eight hundred elephants, just to make sure.

When I went back into the shop, she was gone. Her bin bag was on the desk, messing up my jigsaw, and one of the twins was on my case.

"Dan! We were looking for you! Where did you get to?"

"I was out the back. I suddenly felt a bit sick," I said.

Was I lying?

"Are you alright now? Because some lady just brought in a few things for you to sort, if you feel up to it."

Some lady. Right.

"Feeling better now, thanks," I replied, unable to stop staring at the bag on the desk.

"There's a sack full of baby clothes under the counter as well," she said, her voice dropping to a whisper. "It's really better if you sort those, too. My sister…"

She trailed off, but I was gone before her, following the elephants.

"Fine," I said, not really listening.

I ripped the bag open and scoured through it, searching for clues. Everything within it was well-handled and vague. A table lamp, a teapot. A pair of curtains, a wall clock. Old clothes that were new to me – nothing I could remember ever seeing her in. Then I found it at the very bottom, a pearl amongst all the shit. A bright blue shirt. I lifted it out carefully and held it up to my face. It smelled of nothing but detergent, smelled nothing like my father.

"Do you like it, Alfie?" she'd asked, as he held it up in front of the bay windows for inspection. It was Christmas morning and I was eight or nine years old. A year made all the difference then, but it's not so any more. I was wearing the clothes that I'd slept in and sat amongst all the wrapping paper like some happy tramp. I'd opened all my presents already, then graciously allowed the adults to take the floor.

"It's…it's a nice colour," he replied, gruff and un-fancy as ever.

"It's topaz," she replied. And at that, I loved it for him. Topaz was a jewel and jewel thief movies were my favourites.

He learned to love it too, when he saw it through my eyes. It became his Saturday best, worn down the Miner's Welfare for the afternoon session. Sometimes I would go with him, take shy sips of his bitter when he allowed it, lean back into the crook of his armpit feeling lightheaded. Burying myself away, hiding out from the colliers. Often they would come to the club directly after the morning shift down the pit, still slathered in black coal dust and blue humour at three o'clock in the afternoon. They would leer down at me with their darkened faces, ruffle my hair with their filthy hands. Steal my crisps and then hand me compensatory five pence pieces, which I would snatch away from them vengefully.

I hated them coming over to the table, because they took him away from me. But the dark shapes take everyone away, eventually. When he died, I had no one to cling onto and nowhere left to hide.

I folded the shirt away and placed it gently in a drawer. Shoved all the other items to the edge of the desk contemptuously and grabbed the sack of baby clothes from under the counter. Next. Old death and new life together, both bagged up and waiting to be broken down.

22nd April 2016

From: danroberts@h–mail.com

To: amonsafari@whizzymail.com.au

RE: Stink

Dear Amber,

Do I stink?

I realise that's quite an opening gambit, maybe the most abrupt I've heard since I was approached by a moped-riding tour guide at a cafe in Hue, Vietnam. He sauntered up to my breakfast table with a roll-up hanging out of his mouth and said this:

"My name is Bill. I worked with American GIs during the war. I saw some things. Some nights I can't sleep."

Why, good morning to you too, sir. Take a knee, soldier! Help yourself to a pastry. Try to avoid the *madeleines*, though. They might trigger an unpleasant flashback.

I haven't got any sense of smell, so the question of odour is frequently a concern of mine. I chuck all my clothes in the backpack, they get jumbled together and then I don't know what's clean and what's dirty anymore. So, in selecting an evening's ensemble I tend to do a quick *eeny-meeny-miney-mo* prostration before a pile of apparel, spray whatever wins through with half a can of Lynx and head out.

I was in a hostel common area in San Francisco once and I had the unsettling notion that people were gravitating away from me as though I were a suspect device. It's not nice when people do that, is it, Amber? I put my head down, trying in vain to catch even the faintest whiff of my own man musk. When I looked up again my friend Fabio had entered the room and was watching me. Unfortunately, I still had the neck of my T-shirt across the bridge of my nose.

"What the fuck are you doing?" he asked.

"Do I...smell bad?" I asked.

He leaned in close and sniffed.

"Nothing too problematic," he shrugged.

We had arrived in San Francisco a few hours before, both completely unaware that we were just in time for the start of Gay Pride week. Our first stroll through the city was to be an eye-opener. The best part of Gay Pride is actually the day before the parade – they have this big trade fair in some park. All the companies are anxious to appear gay-friendly and court the pink dollar, so each has a stall handing out promotional goods. Fabio and I came away with two big carrier bags full each – boxer shorts, T-shirts, Frisbees, condoms, hair gel, moisturiser, key rings, pens...and an apple. As a staunch Catholic from Brazil, he was somewhat perturbed by some of the sights he saw during Pride. But as a tight backpacker, he wasn't going to turn down any freebies.

He gave me his apple though, lest it was impregnated with homosexuality. On the way back to the hostel, we stopped in a local bar for a sundowner. Three American girls seated in one of the pub's booths were inspecting us with mild interest until they looked down at our bags and started laughing amongst themselves. The motif on the outside of the bags was an advert for "Elbow Grease Personal Lubricant."

Fisting cream.

That was about the end of my time with my *companheiro* Fabio. He flew home in disgrace from there, back to Rio to confess his sinful associations to the giant dashboard Jesus atop Corcovado Mountain. When I saw him off at the airport, he handed me his new Bible, a Portugese–English dictionary. Inside he'd inscribed a message in his inimitable style of diction:

To my big friend Dan...

We'd first met as roommates in Las Vegas and then travelled all the way through California together. In true samurai tradition, we became each other's retainers. In the first instance, he saved my life by performing an intervention when some wanker from Essex slipped an LSD blotter into my Mountain Dew. Later, naked and under its influence, I attempted to jump into the hostel's swimming pool from the balcony of our dorm room at 4am. It can happen in Vegas. We were only on the second floor, but when I looked at the projected trajectory angle the next day, I realised Fabio's instincts had been correct.

I located the kid from Essex the next day, in the very same pool, where I greeted him warmly by the scalp. You wouldn't imagine that someone from Canvey Island would panic so much about a little water in his lungs.

"He cried with a lady face," Fabio later observed. Then we were close.

Further down the line in Los Angeles, he fell sick with a strong fever and I repaid the debt by nursing him back to health. Meaning I brought him the odd bowl of soup and took him to the doctors. I didn't mop his fevered brow and sing him lullabies.

I haven't spoken to Fabio for over a year now, but I know we're still close. Someday soon, I'll make it over to South America, and when I get to Rio de Janeiro I'll receive the hero's welcome his family promised me for looking after their boy when he took ill. Then we'll pick up exactly where we left off. Some people you meet on the road fall by the wayside, but some people never leave you, even when they're somewhere else.

And some people just stink.

Dan.

Amber: Euthanizing Toddlers

"Once, in Art Class, they gave us all pieces of graph paper with a hundred squares on it. We had to draw our favourite thing one hundred times," I tell Dan. "I drew one hundred bowls of spaghetti."

"I don't...I don't even know what you'd have me do with that information, Amber," he replies.

We're in Pickwick's Bar, lazing around after a good lunch. Obviously, I had the spaghetti. Again. You can't go wrong with the spaghetti. It's a grotty old couch we're sat on, but it feels like it's ours. Dan's got his arm around me, stroking my hair as I lay my head against his chest. He's a little bit sweaty but...it's Africa, eh? Better to be here with a stinky man than a man who stinks.

The only thing spoiling the vibe is this little girl who keeps running around the place like a loony. Her parents are concentrating on their food and occasionally glance over at her in an *isn't-she-adorable* kind of way. No, she fucking isn't. They shouldn't let kids into bars anyway, not unless there's a ball-pool or something for them to play with.

A whirlpool would be a better option for this one.

Now she's in front of us, banging her bottle of juice on the table again and again. I had a few glasses of wine and a good root last night and each knock registers as a dull blow to the side of my head. And I know all too well what they feel like.

I can feel Dan's body stiffen next to mine and when I look up at him, he's scowling a little more with each bang on the table's surface. Finally, the girl's parents look around and read the expression on his face in an instant.

"Is she bothering you?" asks the father, in an accent I can't place.

"Yes," says Dan, as I am politely shaking my head no, but meaning the same thing.

They coo and beckon to her, but she is too set upon her mission to smash Cape Town to pieces one bar at a time. If I acted like that in Sydney they'd put me on Pubwatch. Actually, I am on Pubwatch in Sydney, but that's a different story. And I've got a lifetime ban from The Cheesecake Factory for tipping a Black Forest Gateau into Lozzer's hat when she fell asleep on Melbourne Cup Day.

Finally, the father rises from his chair, mightily pissed off at the idea of tending to his own kid. He hoists her away and then the crying starts. She's got one of those chesty coughs that children always get and it makes her wails sound guttural, like a dingo with its paw caught in a trap.

"They should put them in kennels when they go on holiday," whispers Dan into my ear, making me quiver with his sweet talk.

"Do you want...I mean, do you like kids?" I ask him, lifting his hand and inspecting his fingernails as though they might vouch for his genes.

"Dunno," he replies. "They're just so...constant. Do you?"

I think of Neville, repeatedly asking me why I couldn't get pregnant. Think of what happened the last time he asked. Then the kid stops crying and the rinsed out silence brings me back to the present. Dan is already smoothing away the goose-pimples that have appeared on my upper arm without comment. How's that for attentive? Occasionally I pick a good 'un. But mostly not. Eat enough curry and you're bound to swallow the odd cardamom seed though, just like Lozzer always says.

"It'd have to be with the right person," I say. "But I do like kids."

I glance over at the bratty girl, who seems to be hyperventilating now. As a trained healthcare professional, I should probably intervene. But I am on holiday.

"Not that one so much, though," I add. "I could happily suffocate that one."

"Me too," says Dan, laughing. "I would put strychnine in her sippy-cup."

Oddly, I think this might be the closest we've ever been, as we bond over the mooted murder of this child.

His hand glides over my back and comes to rest with his thumb in the back of my kegs. It feels nice when he does that, even though it's quite dirty really. Sexy-dirty, I mean: I'm not saying that I haven't washed my bum.

I sink back down into his body and delight in his chest wobbling as he chuckles. I'm going under willingly.

To be with the right person...

11th May 2016

From: danroberts@h-mail.com

To: amonsafari@whizzymail.com.au

RE: Heart

Dear Amber,

It's me. Dan.

You may remember me from such shows as "Cape Town" and such no-shows as "Everything Since." I never did get picked up after the pilot. I'm starting to wonder if you ever really existed now, like those trucker's stories of the spectral hitch-hikers, an Antipodean apparition, the ghost in the machinations of my Lariam-addled mind.

Today I turned the house upside down looking for a travel insurance policy (regarding the issue of my purloined camera) until I had the wild notion that it might be somewhere in my backpack. Accordingly, I removed Patty Hearst from her closet, where, much like myself, she slumbers *in stasis* until reactivated for the next trip. I never did find the document I was looking for, but I did find my travel journal. Have a sick bucket at hand lest you "chunder" (to use the quaint parlance of your continent), here's an entry from after we met:

"I like the arch of her back, as she pins her hair up in the morning. I like how she burbles her words when she gets excited. I liked it when she asked a waiter for Savlon, rather than Sauvignon. I don't like how her hair falls into her eyes occasionally – they should never be obscured, it's like glimpsing a tiger through the slats of a wicker laundry basket. I don't like how she takes too long in the bathroom or when she finally fights our magnetic pull and ventures that maybe we should get up – diluting ourselves with other people in an effort to be cordial.

"Last night she cried. She cried because she was tired and nervous and upset by a troublesome ex-boyfriend, whose shadow she was outrunning. I held her tight until she stopped, whispering any stupid thing I could think of in her ear until she finally laughed. I could now easily devote my life to making this stranger smile. I can feel myself grow taller in the light that radiates from her when she does. Should this go nowhere, then at least I can say that I once was somewhere. With her. If all of our promises amount to nothing, I will still be forever indebted to her for jumpstarting my heart."

End transmission.

A Northern Englander trying to write romantic prose is akin to you training to be an ice sculptor on the Gold Coast. Hang on, the phone's ringing...oh, that was Mills and Boon. In the funereal wake of that extract, they would like to schedule a public flogging for me. Catherine Cookson will don a gimp mask and wield the cat o' nine tails. Then, afterwards, Dame Barbara Cartland will smear pink desiccated coconut into my wounds as a salve.

My *fingers* were gagging as I typed out that extract. Why not cut and paste it and pass it around at your next barbie? You and your mates can chortle over it between mouthfuls of mudfish. You've been laughing at me for quite a while now already.

You didn't jumpstart my heart, Amber. You hotwired it. Then you drove it around for a while until you got bored, crashed it into the wall of a Netto carpark, fucked off with the stereo, slashed the seats and burned it out. You didn't break my heart, because the word "break" is a verb, and that would imply some level of action that you are now incapable of. At best, we accidentally collided in Cape Town and you dented my heart. A typically lacklustre commitment from you, like you limply swung at it with a Bluebird Toffee hammer.

In truth, I don't know what you did to my heart but at least I can say I've got one.

I also found the parting gift you gave me. Do you remember it? Two fluffy little koala bears, affixed together by Velcro. Aptly, today I could only find one. It's not a bad visual representation of you really, adorable, but with an inherent streak of viciousness.

I took your stupid little fucking koalas out into the backyard, doused them in lighter fluid, and set them on fire. They burned away all too quickly and quietly, leaving me unsatisfied still.

You're at home by now probably, back amongst the sun-bronzed Jackos and Bennos and Tommos of Manly Beach. All those zinc-nosed Princes of Lightness who doubt even the existence of doubt. You don't need to be keeping in with some pasty–faced, potbellied paranoiac at the other end of the world. But always know you could have at least said goodbye.

I won't ever darken your inbox again.

Dan.

Dan: Dicks

I was walking between the charity shop and the retirement home this afternoon. Being semi-unemployed, I am now able to visit my Grandma daily. Because it's never a full day for me until someone I love ignores me.

As I headed down through the estate, passing a tokenistic single mother in the bus shelter, feeding bits of a Greggs' pasty to her child, I approached a T-junction. It was at exactly this moment that I saw a bloke I used to work with, Dick, heading down the intersecting road before me in his car.

I realised that I hadn't seen him in ages, and then in a flash I remembered that he owed me money.

I suspected this was probably why I hadn't seen him in ages.

Money's tight for me at the moment so I didn't want to miss this opportunity to reclaim a debt. I ran out into the middle of the secondary road to see him speeding away. I began shouting his name as loudly as I could and waving my arms about wildly to attract his attention in the rear view mirror. He didn't see me. Or perhaps he did, but elected not to respond to my entreaties.

People do that.

I sighed dejectedly and decided it would probably be a prudent idea to move out of the middle of the road at some point.

As I turned to go back to the pavement, I was confronted by the sight of the single mother, newly emerged from the cocoon-like domicile of the bus shelter. She wore bukkake combats and had a face full of piercings, like the inside of a clockmaker's drawer. Half a car stuck in her head yet she's waiting for the bus. I wondered for a while why she was regarding me in such a puzzled fashion. Then as I recounted my movements, it dawned on me that from where she was stood she had not viewed the passing car. All she had seen was me walking past her mere moments before as an apparently upstanding citizen, before suddenly flipping out and running out into the middle of a road, gesticulating wildly, and all the while shouting:

"DICK! DICK! DICK!"

After this somewhat embarrassing incident, I returned home to draw up a list of all the people who owe me money.

An interesting name came up.

INCIDENT REPORT
COMPLAINANT: Dan Roberts
LOCATION: Monteverde, Costa Rica.

When I walked back to the hostel I could still see the lava trails from Arenal volcano. It looked like the sky had stigmata. The heat in the town was no less insidious. Eleven in the evening and you'd still need to take your shirt off to have a shit.

I was staying in an end terrace of an ugly block of rooms, each one divided by latticed wicker walls. They were so thin you could hear other people's dreams. I returned home from a heavy night's sobriety and switched on the room's fan to slice up the meaty air. It was old enough to look like it belonged on a private eye's desk. It rattled. Initially, I found that annoying. But as I lay back on my sweat-marinated bed the rhythmic quality lulled me away to sleep, as though I were in some hectic womb.

I was awoken some hours later by a knock at the door. Plastered in sleep, I struggled to locate my clothes. By the time I opened it there was no one there.

I went to the toilet and returned to the wrong stalag. Saw someone else exiting the room I thought to be mine. We bumped into each other and both coughed up hairball apologies. I didn't see his face, but a shaft of light illuminated a tattoo on his forearm. It was a representation of Jesus Christ or Che Guevara or Bob Marley or Bob Monkhouse or someone else. I was never entirely sure.

I circuited back around by the toilet and realised that I wasn't mistaken. He *had* been coming out of my room.

I hurried inside and checked my possessions. Nothing was missing, but something felt different. I realised that the fan had been switched off. I stared at the still blades for still minutes as I processed the extent of this violation.

I considered switching the fan back on but in truth, the room was noticeably cooler by then, thanks to the red mist I could almost see seeping under the doorway. Out of it, the Brigadoon of bile was rising in my throat.

I was in a fugue state. I walked out to the next room with the intention of rapping politely at the door and instead watched myself kick it open. Inside, I saw a figure shoot upright in the darkness. I ran towards him, swinging punches wildly before I'd even arrived. My first contact smashed into the side of his head and even in the dark, I could almost see wax flying out of his ear. I jumped on the bed and straddled him, managed to pin his flailing arms down with my knees.

I only stopped swinging when the light came on. I looked down at the roughed up face of a nobody, not the somebody I was looking for at all. The bloke I was seeking was then behind me, his hairy forearm closing round my neck in a sleeper hold and the last face I saw before I blacked out was Jesus or Che Guevara or Bob Marley or Bob Monkhouse scowling at me beatifically.

When I woke up I was back in my own room with a Post-It note stuck to my pounding head.

Go, it said.

My bag had been packed for me and the fan had been removed. When I entered the hallway, the door to the next room was ajar, with the key still in the lock.

I didn't remember everything about the incident. A Post-It, some punches, a tattoo. Two weeks later, in a mucus coloured departure lounge in Nicaragua, I would feign incredulity as a group of excitable Canadians filled in the blanks, told me about *some crazy dude who just went, like, totally nutzoid* in some hostel where they stayed in Costa Rica. The guy I hit, and hit, and hit, it turned out he was from Manchester. A neighbour of sorts, but the wrong neighbour. He limped into a taxi immediately after the assault, probably rode it all the way back to Piccadilly station.

The guy with the tattoo was Israeli. He'd been staying in a room *across* the hall. He'd just finished his National Service, where he'd excelled as a keen student of *Krav Maga* martial arts. Sometimes it's better when you don't find what you're looking for.

About me, little was known. But I have always been low-key and well hidden.

"Some people," I said, when the Canadians had finished their story.

Amber: In the Hands of Men

"I don't think I can do this, Dan."

We're stood at the foot of Table Mountain, watching the cable-car head down towards us. It's a wonderfully sunny day and we are about to die.

"It's not like it's some rickety ski-lift," he says. "It looks pretty big. Pretty hefty."

"That makes it worse, though! It's big and hefty and it'll be full of…" I look around at the people in the queue and lower my voice. "Big and hefty people."

"We could always hike up," Dan replies, squinting towards the sun. "If you really can't do it."

I follow his gaze and view the craggy mountain face before us.

Fuck that.

Next thing I know I'm inside the cable-car. I move straight into the middle, knees knocking together as I walk. I try to grab hold of the central pole to stabilise myself, but my hands are so sweaty they slide down it and I have to keep moving them back up again, like

I'm playing one-potato, two-potato with myself. It all looks quite vulgar. Dan is beside me; as am I.

"Do you want to stand by the window?" he asks. "See the view?"

"Evidently not," I reply, testily. "There'll be a view at the top, won't there?

He nods, looks disappointed but stays where he is, cranes his neck to try to see out of the window. I can never enjoy the sights from one of these things. I always just stare down at the ground, try to calculate the exact height when we'll reach terminal velocity. Then I imagine how we'll die when it falls. In this case, I reckon when the car hits we're all going flying up toward the roof and sixty-five maximum capacity necks will snap in unison, like a box of matches under a crusher.

Dan smiles at me, but I can see the concern in his eyes. I attempt a smile back, but my mouth is so dry that my bottom lip scrapes along my teeth, like a dead bird, after smashing into a patio window. He's yammering something about the tensile strength of the cable, something he's probably memorised from the pamphlet he read in the line.

"Could you," I interrupt. "Could you just hold my hand, please?"

"Oh," he says. "Okay."

I hesitantly free a hand from the pole I've been wanking off and he takes it in his. I feel better then. I don't even mind the clamminess. It holds us together, like Evo-Stik.

Once we get to the top I'm fine. Dan disappears into the shop at the Visitor Centre for something and I walk out to the lookout point, away from the crowd, as far toward the edge as I dare. I try to focus on the view, but I'm distracted by these strange brown creatures that are scurrying around on the mountainside beneath me. I don't even know what they are, they look a bit like that gopher-thingy from *Caddyshack*, except they're fatter and they don't dance. I grow tired of them and turn my attention toward Cape Town. It's all spread out before me like a Monopoly board. I extend my arm and squeeze the tallest building, then usher the tide in and out with a flick of my fingers. I am a God! I should be holding a staff!

The last time I went up a mountain was just outside of Sydney, the Blue Mountains. Neville was supposed to be taking me out for the day, but he'd been out drinking with the footie lads the night before and was in no condition to drive. We ended up taking my car, him by turns surly and snappy in the passenger seat. We bickered when he said that the voice on my GPS system was gay.

"You're always putting people into boxes," I told him.

"That's where some people belong," he replied, pointing to the GPS. "Anyway, that is a box."

Got me on a technicality, there.

We took the easiest pathway, the Princes rock walk to the lookout point. I remember it, had been up there before with my Dad and our dog, Benchy. But, even then, Neville lumbered behind in his hungover state. I got tired of waiting for him and steamed ahead. I made it to the top twenty minutes before he arrived, even though I'd somehow ended up carrying the eskie. Packed with the sandwiches I'd made for Neville and the beer I'd bought for Neville, on this great day out he was supposed to be taking me on.

I'd passed a group of hikers on my way up, but there was no one at the top. No whinging Poms, no loud North Americans, no Japanese tilting their heads and flicking peace signs at the camera. No Neville, not in that moment at least. Nothing but quiet. I went over to the edge and sat down on the eskie. The view wasn't the best. Hazy, the sun still elbowing its way through the crowd of clouds as it headed to the main stage. I listened only to the sound of my breathing, heavy at first from the walk, then gradually achieving its own peaceful rhythm.

A pair of hands closed on my shoulders, jerking me forward and then pulling me back.

"Gotcha!" shouted Neville.

"What is your fucking issue, Neville?" I screamed, jumping up from the icebox with a start. "I'm sat...I'm sat at the edge of an...an *abyss*. What makes you think that's an appropriate thing to do here?"

"Jeez, it was only a joke, babe," he protested, fishing a beer out of my vacated seat and parking himself on a tree stump. "No need to get hormonal about it."

"Why do you have to ruin everything?" I asked, the thin air making me reckless. Ruin me, and a perfectly good mountain.

He didn't say anything. We sat there for another ten minutes in silence. Not the nice kind, not like before his arrival. Neville nursing his difficult first beer, me with my cigarette. You're not even supposed to smoke up there. I only lit it to get back at him. He never liked me smoking, it didn't fit in with his plans for me as a baby-vessel. On the way back down, he steamed ahead of me, carrying the eskie, his attempt to claw back Man-Points for the poor showing on the way up.

I knew that part of him wished he had just pushed me over the edge. I knew it because part of me wished he had too. I followed the trail downhill at a leisurely pace, wishing it would wind on forever.

He was sat on the hood of my car waiting. When I walked across, grasping for the keys in my bag, he bashed me in the jaw and grabbed them. He drove us back home, with the GPS switched off and sports talk radio turned all the way up. I held my tongue for the entire journey, running it instead across the latest contusion in my mouth, a cold can of Toohey's Extra pressed to my cheek.

I feel a hand tapping me on the shoulder.

"Get the fuck away from me!" I blurt, whirling around to see Dan, who's stumbling backwards. He drops the two bottles of water he was holding.

"Jesus, Amber," he says, looking shocked, confused.

"I'm so sorry," I reply, moving towards him. "I was...I was miles away."

<u>25th May 2016</u>

From: <u>danroberts@h–mail.com</u>

To: <u>amonsafari@whizzymail.com.au</u>

RE: Whoa!

Dear Amber,

Whoa, now, hang on a minute! Stop the clock! Just exactly what kind of a mug do you take me for? I bet you thought you'd made the perfect, clean getaway, didn't you? But don't break your arm patting yourself on the back just yet, because I'm onto you now.

You owe me money.

You've really outdone yourself this time. Just when I thought you couldn't possibly sink any lower in my estimation, you go from the Marie Celeste to the Marie Rose all in one week. This is right down there with stealing one of those Sooty charity boxes out of a pub, or joyriding on a mobility scooter. And I had genuinely forgotten all about it too, until a certain event today jogged my memory.

Is that what this has been all about? You'd rather hang onto a measly amount of money than ever speak to me again?

Obviously, it's not enough that hordes of you Australians head over to work in London every year, berate the weather and the people and the beer for the duration of your stay, rape our economy for six months and then use the money to bankroll your Big Trip around the more scenic areas of Europe. We've always been accepting of that. We view it as an appropriate recompense for days gone by when we sent you the diseased rabbits, overly fertile blackberries, Hale and Pace and The Proclaimers. It's the very least we can do.

You've always been more than welcome here – because, realistically, no English person is ever going to last more than five minutes working in the hellish environment of a Walkabout pub, subserviently doling out ostrich burgers and alcopops to plasterers and their atrophied wives on Family Allowance date night: She's got love-bites on her neck that look like the onset of meningitis, blown glass clown figurines in her alcoves and a satellite dish above her rotisserie vent.

"Ugh," she says. "I don't know if I can eat this, Daz."

He's got a Celtic cross on his arm and a thwarted dream of breeding Weimeraners.

"It's just like a chicken with long legs, Kayleigh," he replies.

But he's really looking at you and not her, skimming you over, trying to impress you with his *papier* wit. He's thinking that when you ask him what he'd like for dessert, he might cock an eyebrow like a terrier's leg and say:

"How 'bout you?"

But he probably won't, he knows what it is to wake up on the naughty couch, then head out to work with its corduroy lines still imprinted upon his face.

So we need you for that. But now you have to take the money right out of our pockets? Shame on you.

Here's a brief recap in case you have any doubts about the veracity of my claim: It was our last full day together in Cape Town, a Sunday. Your bankcard wasn't enabled yet. You had American dollars but all the exchanges were shut. I lent you 600 rand.

We didn't have such a big night, just the meal at Ocean Basket (where we shared the Solemate platter, and how I wish to Christ's pustulated wounds I'd forgotten that part). So, just before we went back to the hostel you gave me your last 180 rand back.

"You don't have to do that," I said.

"I hate owing people money," you replied. "I promise I'll send you the rest as soon as I get home. Or you can come and collect it."

But you made a lot of promises that you didn't keep in Cape Town, eh, Amber?

All told, that's a total outstanding balance of 420 South African rand. I checked on a currency conversion website today and in sterling it comes to £36.24.

Or, for cash, we can call it £36.24.

I don't know what that is in your beer-proof money, I couldn't find an option to change it into that on the page I looked at. Not surprising really, it's hardly like Australia is a global superpower, is it? It probably never will be until the day that dust becomes a valuable trading commodity, or some social paradigm shift makes barbequing a covetable skillset. Be sure to let me know if there's anything here that you disagree with. How would I like my money?

Promptly.

Dan.

Dan: The Rattled Sabre

The last woman who stole from me was my mother, when she took my father away. Her need to be kept in the lack of style she had grown accustomed to yanked my Dad out of his desk job in the colliery. He went back down into the pit he had left for health reasons, where the overtime was. Twelve months later, he was all out of hours, dead from emphysema. Ashes to ashes.

He went underground out of love for a woman and ever since I reached adulthood I've been going over ground out of hatred for her. I went away because…well, I went away because I did something bad, but I also wanted her to feel my absence, so she would know how it was to have someone you love taken away from you suddenly. But she was too drunk to even notice I was gone.

I try not to think of my mother, in the same way that she never thought of me. I try not to think of my father in the last year of his life, with all the tubes and the oxygen tank. They were there to help him, but as a child I saw those tubes as straws draining a milkshake. My most abiding memory of my father in happier times is seeing him at play with Sabre, our bull terrier, a breed of canine renowned for its tenacity and strength. My dad used to rag the dog about at the end of a manky old towel, with the dog clinging on for dear life. Dad wasn't well even then; as soon as he had grown breathless he would hang the towel up on the rotary washing line, with the dog's teeth still gripped onto it. The beast would stay there, suspended in mid-air, until we took pity on it and lured it back down to ground with cold cuts.

Dad went into the family plot. Mother fell into a gin bottle. Broken-hearted Sabre bit the bailiff who was taking away my father's armchair and went on a one way trip to the vets.

But I'm still here. I am as tenacious as that terrier, dogged in my determination, and I will never give up until the money that is owed to me is repaid.

Amber: Mongrels

I wake up in Dan's bed and he's not there. For some reason, I've never felt so alone in my entire life. I jump out of the sheets and throw one of his T-shirts on, inhaling his scent as it passes over my nose. Still a bit sweaty, if I'm honest. I'm wandering around the hostel looking for him when it dawns on me that I haven't got any knickers on. What a total slut! I check myself in a glass door to make sure nothing's hanging out.

Clear.

The door is marked TV Room, which is the last place I'd expect to find Dan unless the telly is locked onto National Geographic or The History Channel or something worthwhile and boring like that. I peek inside anyway.

There's one person sat in there, with his back to me. I recognise him from the shape of his head. Like a breadfruit. It's Peter/Dieter the German. He's holding out the remote, flicking through the channels, snickering snottily at everything he sees. I'm just about to back out of the room before he notices me when the channel changes again and I see *him*. There on the screen, there for me just like he always was and always will be.

Not Dan, of course. Benji.

Peter/Dieter brings up the remote again and it suddenly looks like a detonator in his hand. I don't want to let him know I'm in the room, but I have to say something. I try to phrase it as delicately as possible.

"Don't you *dare* push that fucking button!" I shout, pulling up a chair in front of the screen, only just remembering to shut my legs when I feel the draught that comes with his stare.

When I was a little girl, I wanted to be a dog. Or, to be more specific, Benji. I would watch videos of his adventures over and over again; make him race through forest fires and face down mountain bears until the tape whined. My parents, tired of sitting through these films again and again, encouraged me to see other dogs. Lassie, Hambone and Hillie, The Littlest Hobo, even Rin Tin Tin. None of them interested me. Especially not Lassie. That stuck up bitch, always with her beautiful coat blowing in the wind at the top of a hill like some shampoo commercial.

"Benchy," I would say. "I want Benchy."

Benchy never wore a collar, but if he did it would have been blue. Benchy was the every-dog, the plucky under-person who fought back.

It wasn't long before I wanted a real one. Like most loved and spoilt only-children, I learned to nag before I could talk. It took me six months of campaigning to get what I wanted. The biggest obstacle, understandably, was my mother's allergy to dogs. I would concoct imaginary potions to combat it with my tea set and bring them to her in bed every morning. At 5am.

There was a screening process. We would tour Sydney's dog shelters and my mother would enter each animal's chamber and hover there nervously until she sneezed or the dog bit her or both.

The dog I ended up with didn't look much like Benchy. Even as a pup, he was kind of a big oaf, borderline retarded (and that's going some by dog standards) and clumsy. He never raced through forest fires or faced down mountain bears, but he did run a possum out of the yard once. I bathed him with kisses on that day, then bathed him properly when I discovered how he tasted.

I loved him anyway. He was my constant companion, the daily annoyance of school the only time we were ever separated. I had no interest in playing with other children once home, even less in sharing Benchy with them. He was mine, I would growl when others came near him. There are browned-over photos in which I am eating my food from a plate set down on the ground next to his bowl. My dinner date, the first man in my life other than my father. The first man I slept with. Not in a sexual way, obviously. He was a dog. He's the reason I wanted to become a veterinarian and somehow ended up as a nurse. I'm still patching up mongrels and galahs, though. In later life, I was drawn to boys, then men, who I thought had the same qualities as him. I found them all lacking. None of them ever measured up to Benchy.

When he died I...

When he died I...

I'm stammering again. This is the point where the TV anchor wipes away a tear. Rolling news. More on this top story later. It was possibly the saddest day of my life, but it also reminds me of something and someone else. Someone I came here to Africa to forget.

"Again you are being provocative to me, Amber," says Peter/Dieter, interrupting, dragging me away from my own heart.

"Aw, do fuck off, mate," I say, grabbing the RC from him and doubling the volume.

1st June 2016

From: danroberts@h–mail.com

To: amonsafari@whizzymail.com.au

RE: Hippos

Dear Amber,

At Croc Valley campsite in Zambia, I stumbled bleary-eyed out of my tent in the middle of the night to visit the toilet, blissfully unaware that I had just walked within inches of a grazing hippopotamus. It was only the sweet relief of nocturnal urination that sharpened my senses and retuned my ears to the beast's loud crunching. After I had reassured myself that it was too large an animal to fit through the WC doorframe, I settled in by the outbuilding's cracked window and watched this magnificent creature take its leisurely evening meal. In truth, I didn't have much choice in the matter – there was no way I was chancing getting past it again.

It dined with a Spaniard's appetite and lack of urgency, and so for forty minutes I was held hostage in a piss-dripping, mosquito-riddled African khazi by a hippopotamus, a mere thirty feet from my own temporary home. And yet it was one of the greatest experiences of my life.

No doubt you went on a few game drives yourself during your Overland tour in Africa. I expect your guide tutored you well in the ways of the hippopotamus, quoting that hoary old statistic about how hippos kill more people each year than lions or crocodiles or chlamydia or whatever it is. No doubt they also instructed you never to come between a hippo and the water and never, ever come between a hippo and its young.

By the same token, if your future travels should ever bring you to these fair shores (perhaps to retrace the footsteps of your equally larcenous ancestors – and do be sure to let me know when your flight touches down, I'll guide you in with a laser pointer and meet you amidst the wreckage) you will come to know one truth: NEVER come between a Yorkshireman and his money. Some people still say "thee" and "thou" around here, Amber, so don't think for a second that our wrath isn't equally Old Testament.

From your obvious lack of morality, I'll assume you're not familiar with The Old Testament. That's the part of the Bible where men were men and fatted calves were worried; the bit where God wasn't afraid to knock a few heads together to get what he wanted. God was like a renegade cop who played by his own set of rules. But the sequels are never as good, so things tapered off a bit with the New Testament, because in the interim between the two books some of the archangels got together and formed a PR consultancy.

They looked at focus group feedback of God's initial test screenings and advised him that the "God is a vengeful God" bit wasn't playing too well in the liberal provinces. They workshopped the idea of Jesus as a more people-friendly embodiment of God's brand. Jesus was a poster boy, like Tony the Tiger or Captain Birdseye. He was a naturally gifted raconteur, had a few good parlour tricks and certainly knew his way around a Dado joint, but if he strolled into Doncaster today, he'd be regarded as a trustafarian hippie. People would expect him to lead his disciples around on pieces of string, and fail to be impressed until he had turned their water into Special Brew.

When people ask me if I believe in God, I always say that I don't. But I always whisper it, just in case she's listening. Yes, God would undoubtedly be a woman – because she never returns my calls either. She's always too busy in the executive bathroom, plucking her eyebrows or waxing her ovaries or whatever it is you people do in there for all that time.

I once travelled on a junk boat through Halong Bay, Vietnam, where local legend dictates that its stunning succession of small islands and atolls were formed from the emerald tears of a dragon flying over the sea. By the same token, God's Own Country Yorkshire was formed from the bitter tears of betrayed unionists mixed with the dusty, catarrh-riddled phlegm of swindled miners. All packed down into moorland infused with the pitchforked corpses of robdog land barons. If someone steals from us, we will be relentless in our pursuit of them. And we have excellent topsoil consistency.

Seduced and abandoned by you, and yet I can't do anything about that. There is no legislature for matters of the human heart, no Claims Direct compensation for the cuckolded or the chucked. Sweet nothings are exactly that, whispered words like wind through chimes. Lover's promises can crumble like a pensioner's hips. But a sum of money owed, that's something real and tangible. It's not immaterial. It is material: paper notes folded inside a leather wallet or metal coins banging against a leg through the fabric of a pocket.

I want my money back, Amber. Please contact me immediately to arrange repayment.

I don't doubt that you'll ignore this email as you have ignored every other email I have sent. But I will keep reminding you of this debt on a weekly basis. I'll be as constant as the Northern Star (not entirely sure if you have that in the Southern Hemisphere – it's a big, fuck-off star), the summer cold you just can't shake, or that nagging toothache from too many Anzac biscuits.

See you next Tuesday.

Dan.

Dan: Foot and Mouth

The hits just keep coming. Yesterday, I found a memory card from my stolen camera. In a shoe, of all places. I slotted the card in my laptop to see what was on it.

Fittingly, it was full of lost memories, containing as it did photographs from the meal Amber and I shared at Mama Africa's restaurant on Long Street, Cape Town. The place where we purposely ordered the most disgusting things we could find on the menu. We ate squid heads and snails there, but for some reason she balked at the idea of eating the chicken's feet. In one rose-tinted candid, taken by the waitress, I am trying to force these feet into her mouth as she protests.

Small wonder our relationship had problems.

The formerly devil-may-care bohemian and self-styled wild child Amber Shaughnessy was cowed by a piddling piece of poultry.

"It's just the way it looks," she said to me.

"What, like a foot?"

"Well, yeah, basically."

What did she expect the chef to do, paint its fucking toenails? If she had been just a little bit braver, she might at least have tried one. But then, if she had been just a little bit braver, she would have replied to my emails by now.

In a truly sappy fashion, I looked all through these photos many times. I confess to using the zoom facility to close in on her face. I scrutinized the eyes for underlying signs of doubt. In one picture, Amber was stood behind me and I panned around the frame to see if she were holding a knife, poised to drive it between my shoulder blades. I regarded each of these time capsule images with my finger poised above the delete button. I felt like an assassin. One little click from me to make Amber disappear, just as no little click from her has made me disappear.

All those game drives in Africa, it's really just like going to one of those restaurants where they have photos of the food on the laminated menu. When I got to Cape Town, I ate most of the creatures I had been stalking across the savannah. Springbok, gemsbok, kudu, oryx, zebra, elan, warthog – there's nothing much that can outrun you when it's on a plate.

In China, I ate snake, frog, moth larvae, scorpion and testicles of indeterminate origin. I ate seahorses in a fish restaurant in Nicaragua – I didn't know they were a protected species at the time; in Central America the only protected species are the ones that can load a gun.

I ate camel in Jordan, water buffalo in Cambodia, yak in Tibet, alligator in America, kangaroo in Australia.

I love animals, but by the same token, I'll happily devour the seared flesh of any creature other than man.

I'm not a cannibal; I wouldn't eat anything so spoiled as a human being.

Maybe Amber differs. Maybe that's why she wouldn't eat the chicken's feet.

19th July 2016.

From: danroberts@h-mail.com

To: amonsafari@whizzymail.com.au

RE: Bohemianism

Dear Amanda,

Will you respond to that? Amber's not even your real name, is it? It's just a stage name. Check your Inequity Card. When we were comparing passport mugshots, your dainty thumb wasn't big enough to obscure your true moniker. I refrained from comment at the time, so as to spare your blushes. Because I exercise consideration for the feelings of others; give that a whirl sometime.

Here's another little tip: Next time you reinvent yourself, see if you can turn into someone *better*.

One of the people on my overland trip in Asia was a woman called Namida Lakeside. Needless to say, that wasn't her real name, she'd changed it. Namida is a name derived from the Native American Chippewa tribe, meaning "star dancer". Lakeside is a shopping centre on the outskirts of Doncaster. I doubt that she was aware of the latter fact when she renamed herself, but it did become emblematic of the dichotomy of her character. In her previous incarnation, her given name was Sharon Fothergill.

Sharon Fothergill had been a recently jilted, disillusioned call-centre worker in Swindon. Her boyfriend Tim had broken off his seven-year engagement to her so he could concentrate on his long cherished dream of becoming a professional quad biker. Subsequently depressed by this shock announcement, she had a moment of clarity at work one day, when a customer she was calling informed her that she was little more than a commission based battery hen who could stick her BT broadband package right up her feathered arsehole. Then

Sharon's pips went. She handed in her hands-free headset, cashed in her chipboard vestibule, and clocked out, never to return.

For a fortnight after that, she stayed in her flat, sitting around in gravy and tear-stained pyjamas, drinking Paul Masson's Californian Carafes. "Loose Women" became her breakfast TV, and she habitually took her first libation when "Eggheads" started. To offset the damage caused by all the alcohol, she tried to eat at least one tin of canned fruit every day, taking it from the Harvest Festival donation stockpile in the kitchenette's corner cupboard. One day, when there was only a dusty tin of syruped lychees left, she decided to change her ways.

She took an Alpha Course at a church in Bristol and beta-blockers with her Ovaltine every night. She gained a dubious accreditation as a Life Coach through the internet. She got her roots retouched by deed poll and rented a small office space above a tobacconist's shop. She painted it in warm colours, and plied her trade to the many dispossessed and disenfranchised of Wiltshire. One of her first clients was Tim. His newly acquired crutches made it difficult for him to negotiate the steep stairwell. His power animal turned out to be an otter.

For such a deeply spiritual person, Namida Lakeside could be a snarky cow. The Alpha Course tenets of unity and equality for all didn't extend to anyone bold enough to sit in "her" seat on the Overland truck. Her pathological aversion to washing up after meals was more Jainist in its intensity. Her sense of serenity could often be misconstrued, and most people just thought she was a lazy bastard.

When she joined the group midway through the trip in India, she didn't introduce herself as Namida. She introduced herself as Namida-it's-a-Chippewan-word-meaning-Star-Dancer. But she wasn't so keen on sleeping in her tepee and would upgrade to a hotel room whenever the opportunity presented itself. She was a champagne existentialist, a grouchy anti-materialist in Gucci sunglasses. If, in true Native American tradition, her name had been given to her by the tribal elder rather than herself, it probably would have been Scowling Beaver.

In Leopold's Cafe in Mumbai, our tour leader summoned me over and asked me to welcome the newest group member, Namida. Quick as a flash, she extended her hand and asked me if I knew what her name meant. In fact, I did, as I had already heard her showing off the origin story to the four people she was introduced to before me.

"I think so," I said. "Isn't it a Native American word meaning pretentious?"

It was intended as a joke, but it wasn't well received. Heap bad medicine, around me she was an angry squaw in Maybelline war-paint after that. Later in the trip, I was doing laps in the swimming pool at a hotel in Jodphur when she walked past.

"That's the first exercise I've seen you do on this trip, Dan," she said, smirking.

This from a woman who brings a sick note to get out of wiping a surface down, and once offered me five dollars if I pitched her wigwam for her.

"I'm on holiday, Namida," I replied. "Back home I do manual labour for eight hours every day. I'm not like you. I don't just sit around on beanbags, drinking peppermint tea and encouraging people to emote."

She kicked my towel in the pool.

Outside of Jaisalmer, our group went on a camel safari. All the camels form a convoy, linked together by one long rope. Except for my beast, a scar-faced behemoth named Peacock. The guides informed me that Peacock was a free spirit and could not be tethered to any other creature, needing to roam of his own accord. Obviously, they didn't phrase it exactly like that, in fact it was just a little boy with a mouthful of betel nuts saying:

"Peacock is craaaazy."

Nevertheless, I liked the idea of this, and supported Peacock's innate right to do as he so chose. But, in practice, all it meant was that while the rest of the group moved ahead in formation, I would be constantly looping around them in the erratic manner of Bernie Clifton atop his ostrich, as my ride constantly sought out fresh clumps of desert grass to eat.

The travelling circuit is full of people who remind me of Peacock and Namida. They call themselves free spirits because it sounds more poetic than calling themselves selfish or lazy. Highly critical masses of contradictions: they say they're anti-capitalist, but they didn't obtain that Round the World ticket by trading blankets. They say they hate the police, but when their flat got burgled it wasn't the head shop that they rang. They didn't champion the individual's innate right to freedom of expression when some clucking heroin addict shat in a drawer of their tallboy and then wiped his pallid arsehole on one of their throw rugs. They say they despise the government, but on polling day they were too busy eating Rice Krispies out of a mug and watching a "Game of Thrones" boxset to cast their vote. But hey, that's okay, because it doesn't change anything does it?

You're a flower child that blossomed into a Triffid. Apparently, it's fine to hurt people and treat them like shit. You can get away with it just as long as you're wearing toe rings when you're kicking someone in the teeth.

Dan.

INCIDENT REPORT

COMPLAINANT: Amanda Shaughnessy AKA Amber Shaughnessy

LOCATION: Sydney, Australia.

I get up to clear the plates from the table and Neville grabs my wrist and pulls me back down into my seat. Here we go again. Not so much as a thank you for the meal or anything. Even though I spent hours making it and he shovelled it down his fat pie-hole in minutes. Even though he's still got the gravy on his fucking chin.

"Why can't you get pregnant, Amanda?" he asks.

Because after we have sex I wait until you are asleep then creep into the bathroom and sluice out my insides. Because your baby in my womb would be a hostage situation. Because I'm still taking the birth control pills. I hide them in my locker at work. It's where I keep all my secrets, the only place of mine that is still mine, the only place you can't ransack. If you opened it, the first thing you would see is the empty sellotape frame inside the door. It used to hold a picture of you, Nev. Until I tore it into pieces one day and flushed it down the toilet I sat upon as I cried myself through yet another coffee break.

"D...du..dunno," I say. "It's not always so easy."

"I never had any problems with Jackie," he says.

Neville already has a child, a little boy, but I wouldn't call him a father. Nor did the prosecuting solicitor.

"I... I don't like it when you talk about her," I say. I phrase it like that because I know that jealousy is an emotion he can understand, if not control. But I suppose

I am jealous of Jackie. Because she got away from him, because she's free. I only ever met her once, in a nightclub when I'd just started seeing Neville. She saw me enter with him and collared me in the toilets. Warned me about him, told me he was a mongrel. I laughed it off as sour grapes. Not my Neville. He's sweet as. Couldn't be.

But now I think maybe she was relieved. I was her relief.

"There must be something wrong with you," Neville says, pulling me back towards him with words, for once. Pushing me away from him again with their meaning.

"There's...there's nothing wrong with me," I say, gathering the plates quickly, dumping them in the sink to get away from him. I look out of the kitchenette window toward the beach, feel the cooling breeze on my face, hear the waves. Even the moon and the tide are nudging me back into this room I want to escape from.

"Are you saying it's me?" he asks, his voice raised now. Then he's behind me, gripping my shoulders to turn me around. His thumbs are cold and as sharp as knitting needles, penetrating my back and piercing my heart.

"It *is* you," I reply and fish around in the warm water for something I can use against him. The only thing I can find is a two-pronged corncob skewer. One of those little moulded plastic ones that's actually shaped like a corncob. For easy reference, I suppose, so you don't try and use them for spearfishing.

It'll do. As his brute force whips my body around to face him, I jab it into his neck.

"Fuuuuuck," he says, as though he's deflating. Then he clatters back onto the lino, groaning.

It looks odd, him with that corn cob sticking out of him. Maybe I should ram one in the other side of his neck to balance it out. A Frankenstein's monster for the Cook N'Dine crew. I draw a long knife from the console instead. Then I kneel between his legs, for the last time ever. I watch him gurgling and whimpering for a while, see the dark blood buttering the bright yellow corn. Then I take the knife in both hands and bring it down towards his crotch.

I stop before impact, but he screams anyway. I push the tip of the knife through the button fly of his jeans until it's prodding against his shrinking cock. Neville doesn't wear undies. Fucking bogan.

When I speak, I don't stammer. My voice is calm and level. My voice belongs to someone I'm meeting for the first time tonight.

"You're a violent man, Nev," I say. "But you're weak. Maybe that's what makes you so violent. You can only kill me bit by bit. But I could kill you right now. Cut off your dick and slit your throat. And that's what I will do to you, tonight or one of these nights."

He says nothing, but I've seen those eyes before. With my dog, Benchy, when his back legs finally gave out and he lay next to the front door all day like a draught excluder. My dad carried him out behind the woodshed. His last walk, one of the few I didn't accompany him on. He looked at me like that when Dad picked him up and I just couldn't...

Neville's done.

I stuck a fork in him.

If I'd have known it would be this easy I would have done it months ago. I stand up and toss him a tea towel.

"Get your stuff together and get the fuck out of my flat," I say. Then I open the fridge and pour myself a nice big glass of Savlon, just to spite him. I head over to the couch and switch on the TV. I can hear him lumbering around in the kitchenette, but it doesn't interest me anymore. I drink half of the wine in one gulp and when the glow rises through me, I suddenly feel very tired, like I haven't slept for years.

I wake up a couple of hours later with the TV still on. The knife is wedged in my hand but I've spilt the rest of the wine on the settee. How do you clean white wine stains again? With red wine? No, that can't be right. Maybe it's vinegar, or salt. Fuck it; I'll just buy a new one. All change.

The only trace of Neville is his blood on the linoleum. Nine months together. The length of a pregnancy. I mop it away in seconds and then tidy the rest of the house. At 4am, when I'm finally done, I step into the shower and scrub myself clean. Every flake of dead skin in the plughole feels like a piece of the old Amanda falling away. When I get out, I flick the switch on the extractor fan to spirit the steam away. There's a blue spark and all the flat's lights go off.

Bugger. Just when there's no longer a man about the house. I don't even know where the fuse box is.

It doesn't matter. The sun will be up soon.

I drop the towel and look at myself in the full-length mirror, lit only by the orange glare of the streetlamp outside the frosted window. It coats me in its new glow, blanching out the bruises on my arms and ribs and shoulders and legs.

I am Amber now.

I look good with a bit of colour. Maybe I'll go on holiday.

Dan: Contract Work

I am now a fully qualified forklift driver.

Karen at the Jobcentre, tired of my bi-monthly bleatings of being overlooked by a cold and uncaring corporate world, booked me onto the course to enhance my skillset. I was summarily despatched to a bleak industrial estate on the outskirts of Doncaster, for an orientation session with two other trainees.

When asked for two forms of identification, Andy produced his Jobseekers book and his jailcard. He had been released a mere twelve weeks ago, after a four-year bounce for armed robbery. A slight and affable young man, I later told him that it was hard for me to picture him waving a shotgun into some bank teller's face, screaming:

"THINK OF YOUR CHILDREN! THINK OF YOUR CHILDREN!"

He laughed and told me that it wasn't quite so cinematic, that he had only donned a Spongebob Squarepants mask and knocked over a couple of corner shops, tooled up with his three-year-old son's spud gun.

"Weren't even loaded," he said.

With another child already on the way, he was keen to get the forklift license under his belt rather than a toy firearm, rejoin the workforce and put his past mistakes behind him. As much as I wished him well for the future, I couldn't help but feel that even if he could drive a forklift truck across a milk-pond, it still wouldn't open too many warehouse doors with prospective employers after their initial CRB check.

The other trainee's name was Dougie, a forty-something former skinhead. Being selected for this course was a drag for him, forcing him to cancel contracts for his covert career as a moonlighting roofer. Like Andy, he was also now a reformed character, having fallen in with the wrong crowd at an impressionable age. He had a small National Front emblem and a swastika tattooed on his forearm. He looked like a fascistic version of Popeye. He would colour these tattoos in with a felt tip pen when he was scratching away at Asian family's shingles. Six points for an "N" and four points for an "F", but Dougie now recognised that these were two letters he could stand to lose when he was scrabbling over their tiles.

Amazingly, his newly acquired Bosnian wife has learned to look right through them, and chosen to see instead the veins and capillaries that coursed with the blood pumped from his recalibrated heart.

After we passed the course, Andy had to go visit his parole officer, but Dougie and I went for a celebratory drink in a nearby pub. Over the first pint, he moaned about all the roofing jobs he had been forced to cancel this week just to attend the course. By the fourth, he told me about all the jobs he *used* to do.

He used to hurt people for money. A sub-contractor, brought in to straighten out disputes with the application of violence.

"Sort of like a counsellor, really," he said, nostalgically. "'Cept with weaponry."

Sometimes it was deals gone sour, sometimes it was domestic affairs. Sometimes it was just because someone didn't like someone else's face and thought it might benefit from a re-fit. He applied no judgment to any of these scenarios. He operated on a sliding scale of payment, pertinent to the severity of the punishment and the tools required to complete each job.

"But I never killed nobody," he ventured, drawing deep on his pint of mixed. "Least, not as far as I know."

I listened to him attentively. It seemed important to him that I know he had once been dangerous. It was easier for him to talk of that than keep his gut sucked in. That last remark of his made him an ally of sorts. He rolled a stick-thin prison issue cigarette to proof-stamp his words and regarded me critically.

"So if you ever wanted anything doing. *Anyone* doing...." he trailed. "Me, I'm retired now. Once the back goes you lose yer accuracy. Swing at someone's kneecap with a mallet and miss...well, you could hurt 'em. But I still know people."

"D'you know anyone in Australia?" I asked.

It turned out he did. It seems there's been a gradual diaspora of right-wing types leaving England for those shores over the last two decades. Many of his former skinhead friends, grown tired of the increasing multicultural aspects of English society, had elected to leave. All they had to do was sit out the necessary waiting period for their criminal records to expire first.

I told Dougie about Amber and he tapped his sovereign ring against his pint pot while he considered it.

"No women, no kiddies. That was my only rule back when I was contracting," he said, ruefully. "But the work soon dries up if you make exclusions like that. I could make a phone call…"

I demurred politely, startled. I was still thinking about all those skinheads, Boeing after Boeing full of shiny pates and Ben Sherman shirts. All those tattooed swallows in flight towards the sun. Then I thought about my oldest friend Tommy, how he had left England because he was tired of fighting. For you, Tommy, the war is over. He'd made a new life for himself in…

Sydney.

I thought about the last time I had seen him there and the circumstances that carried me.

I drained my pint of cloudy lemonade manfully.

"I'll take care of it myself," I said.

6th August 2016

___

From: danroberts@h–mail.com

To: amonsafari@whizzymail.com.au

___

RE: Sixth

Dear Amber,

Happy birthday! Did you think that I wouldn't remember? Forget yours, like you forgot mine? I'm not so quick to discard people as you are, sweep them under the rug like Kettle chip crumbs as soon as someone new comes along to the party.

I won't take up too much of your time with this email, as I expect you're busy impaling chipolata sausages on cocktail sticks in readiness for your party. Will it remind you of the way you emasculated me, I wonder? And, to scale as well. Here is a poem I wrote for your special day:

Amber
You are the pubic hair clogging my drain
You are the Vim in my line of cocaine
You are the badger that savaged my brother
You are the safe that fell on my mother.

Have a great day, Amber! Many happy returns!
Dan.

Dan: Chives at Midnight

I lead a small and insignificant life in a small and insignificant place. A mere twelve miles away lies the asbestos jungle of Doncaster. It's quite a big place really, and growing by the day, but here in England we have some archaic law which dictates that a town cannot be reclassified as a city unless it has a Nandos. In Doncaster, the streets are paved with Golden Virginia wrappers, and the first stirring of autumn's winds dislodges all the hypodermic needles from the monkey-puzzle trees.

Over twenty years ago, the closure of the coal-mine tore the blackened lungs from my own town and, to this day, we still struggle to breathe. My Grandmother's house, which I now occupy is, like me, semi-detached. It has a very small garden, but, with its proximity to the countryside, it gets a lot of traffic.

Last night I went out to put something in the bin and found a big ginger cat staring at me. Cats usually hightail it as soon as you come towards them, but this one stood tall, or as tall as a cat can stand, anyway. It watched me warily, but then its eyes were darting about surveying the nearby plant pots.

Obviously, its intended quarry was behind them. I was expecting some wounded bird to splutter out so I was coiled strategically myself. I awaited the kill stroke, readied myself for intervention.

Moments crackled by and then the cat's prey shot out from behind my potted chives. It was a tiny rabbit. I must confess to my shame, having expected some helpless sparrow, I was startled when this ball of fur came darting out. My reflexes failed me and I stood rooted to the spot, watching this defenceless little creature skitter around on the tarmac with the tom in pursuit. I was so mesmerised by what was unfolding in front of me that, before I knew it, the cat had the rabbit in its cavernous ginger maw and was straight off over the fence.

I couldn't sleep at all after that. I lay awake pondering the inherent malice of the feline species. The question that kept coming back to me again and again was this:

Who the fuck do cats think they are?

Dogs are staunch. I know no dog is ever going to split the atom, because they can't even chew a chicken bone without choking, but they're like affable idiots really, aren't they? Canines don't have the perspicacity to get jaded. Chances are you'll never meet a cynical dog. Plus, a dog will give you unconditional love; you could be the biggest arsehole in the world and your dog will still love you.

Conversely, cats don't even seem to like their owners that much. They'll put in the necessary minimum amount of quality time with them, hang around for a while until the kibble's been dished up, and then they're straight out the door, off into the night to harass and slaughter innocents.

They prowl around like snipers, looking for some smaller lifeform to maim. It wouldn't be so bad if they killed to eat – but they do it just for fun. Half the time they don't even finish their prey, just disfigure them and leave them traumatised. Like how the Guerkas wipe out a platoon, but leave one man standing to tell the tale.

Hitler killed between eleven and seventeen million people during World War Two, but British cats claim the lives of an estimated fifty five million birds every year. Cats are furry little sociopaths.

Cats run away when they see humans. It's because they assume that every other creature is as mean spirited and vicious as they are. They think if they give you a chance you'll jump them.

It always makes me laugh when I pick up the local paper – every other week it seems like there's a story about a cat being shot in the eye with a pellet gun or a crossbow (on alternate weeks the victim is either a swan or a duck). Then there's some photo op where a bedraggled looking housing scheme woman is holding up the newly myopic little bastard with a mournful looking expression on her face and horse brasses around her mantelpiece.

"I just can't understand why anyone would do this," said Miss Cawkwell, unemployed, 28. "Malibu is such a gentle cat. He wouldn't hurt a fly."

Today, I went to the supermarket and bought cat food. I bought the brand that 8 out of 10 cats prefer, just to enhance my chances. I didn't need to buy rat poison; you can always find that in old lady's houses; just like you can always find thimbles and doilies. I double dosed the food, dished it up and placed it in the back garden.

Now, as ever, I wait...

And I wrote another poem while I did so:

<u>Cats Are Essentially Cunts</u>:

Cats scowl and hiss
And spray smelly piss
In any dry place they can find
Covertly trained like Bin Laden
To stealth bomb your garden
With shit that can send your kids blind
How do you feature
Such a verminous creature
Could find its way into my home?
To make the world better
I'll reach for my Beretta
And give Snowball two shots to the dome.

Dan: Shonky Dream Sequence

Last night I dreamt we were back on Table Mountain. It was a good, clear day and Amber and I were looking out over Cape Town. We were pointing down towards Camps Bay, trying to locate the exact spot on the promenade where she inadvertently laughed when a fat kid dropped his ice cream cornet. A harbinger of her future cruelty, true, but the lad looked like he could stand to skip the odd dessert. In fact, he looked like he could easily eat two more potatoes than a pig. Amidst this frivolity, and unknown to Amber I had lured her up the mountain with a hidden agenda. I was going to ask her to marry me.

I had the ring all ready and I was going for the traditional approach. Down on one knee, the full palaver. I was nervous, and as I went down, I gave a slight lurch forward and accidentally head-butted Amber in the stomach. It wasn't a killer blow on its own, but, unfortunately, it was enough to knock her off balance and send her straight over the handrail. I rushed forwards expecting to see her plummeting towards her doom, but in fact she had quite flukily landed on a little rock shelf just some twenty-odd feet down.

Other than that little stroke of luck, things weren't looking too good for Amber. Her limbs were arranged at unsettling angles like a pile of pick-up sticks. Amazingly, she still managed to give a little smile. Brave little soldier, Amber. Actually, it was more of a goofy leer; I think she might have been in shock. Then she waved a worryingly slack hand and mouthed the word:

"Yes."

At this point I felt a poll tax riot of emotion – happy that my proposal had been anticipated and accepted, whilst simultaneously looking at her mangled frame and wondering exactly what kind of a wedding dress she would fit into now. Something heavily vented, presumably. I didn't really know whether to call for help or start dropping rocks on her to finish her off.

Then, the dassies began to converge around her limp form.

The dassy has always struck me as quite an amiable little creature, but when they began to eat Amber I realised my impressions of them have been wrong.

Her piercing cries didn't last for too long – I watched stupefied as the alpha male rock hyrax bestrode Amber's sunburnt chest and hoiked out her voicebox with the ruthless efficiency of a gypsy stripping copper cable. At the cessation of her guttural wailing, the less emboldened dassies finally gained the inner courage to approach Amber's prone body and from then on it was sheer carnage; they tore into her like Elk Lodge senior citizens at a Vegas buffet, turned her pretty little face into hamburger meat. Throughout, I stood helpless and inert as these vicious little creatures carried away piece after piece of my fiancé.

After the dassies had taken their fill, there came the birds. Hawks, blackbirds and finally seagulls. It was like a Zorastrian funeral. Amber's shrieks had long since been silenced, but her eyes were still screaming. That is until a crow took one of them away. Just popped it, as you would a spit bubble, and then scarfed it down his neck like an oyster. There wasn't much left of her at all by then. She reminded me of a pulled pork sandwich I had in Fort Worth once. The creatures of Table Mountain dined well on my future wife that day.

I woke up from this hideous dream in a cold sweat. My first thought upon waking: Now how the fuck am I going to get my money back?

Dan: Dead

The call came at 1.30am. As soon as the phone rang, I knew what it was about. I thought that if I didn't answer it then she would still be alive. I pondered the prospect of staying in bed with the pillow held down over my head. Just to buy her a few more seconds on this earth, minutes maybe. But, eventually, common sense relents. When my bare feet touched down on the cold and inhospitable bedroom floor, my Grandma was dead.

It's difficult to watch someone who was once so strong grow so weak before your very eyes. Physical deterioration is an expected part of the ageing process, but what's harder to deal with is the loss of mental faculties. To see a steel-trap mind rusting over, warranty now expired. Back when she was talking, in an hour spent visiting with her, she would often ask me the same questions over and over again. I would feel like one of those oh-so-hard-done-by movie stars at a press junket. Sometimes I would answer the same questions with different answers, testing her to see if she would notice.

She never did.

Often, her mental meanderings were interesting. One moment, she would be berating a contestant on some quiz show, and in the next instant she would be speaking of her time in the munitions factory, or her days in service as a maid at the old mansion house. Time travelling.

So it goes.

And then it went.

It was always thrilling to see her light up momentarily. Witness the synaptic spark, her engine turning over once more – hotwired by a ghost of the person she once was. It backlit her eyes when those images returned to her. But then, just as abruptly, they would be gone. Then she would be all confused again and wondering why the bread bin was hiding from her. All those memories, like marbles rolling around a bagatelle board.

Her condition gradually worsened and finally I had to put her in a home almost a year ago. As I consider this, I'm suddenly recalling that Amber told me she once worked in such a place. And, the last time I saw her, my ghosted *Filipina* Joy Santos was training to work in such a place. It's a unifying theme in the women I have lost.

Everyone always says, "Oh, I won't be any trouble when I get older. Just put me in a home." But when the occasion comes around, I doubt they'll feel the same. It's like putting puppies into a burlap sack and expecting them to sit there compliantly, awaiting the inevitable splash landing in the canal. In Davey Jones' locker, scurvy-souled dead mariners while away waterlogged eternities tossing balls to unwanted terriers. Not all dogs go to heaven.

The home was a nice place and the staff were lovely people, but beyond all the smiles and cups of tea everyone knows that these places are a departure lounge for death. They might as well install one of those ticket machines in reception and have the residents wait for their number to be called. My Grandma didn't always know who I was by this stage, but she at least knew this.

A widow of forty years, a once proudly self-sufficient woman – the indignity of internment was too much for her to take and, accordingly, she began to shut down. There was nothing in her eyes but sadness and resignation when she regarded me then. It was like her pilot light had blown out.

She lived to 83 years of age, and is survived by one grandson who was always far away, even when he was right at her bedside. I asked the attending nurse if she had spoken of me before she passed; if she had spoken at all.

The nurse told me that she had called the name of her last visitor.

Ingrid.

My mother.

Amber: Our Little Chickadee

Dan is dragging me around again. Not to hell and back, but to Stellenbosch. To use his gushing terminology: I don't mind. He's my go-to guy. We go to here, we go to there…I feel like I'm having a more productive holiday thanks to him. Without him, I'd probably just hang around the hostel until it was time to start drinking. And then I'd go to the hostel bar. But now we're moving, passing through the small city on a big bus and heading to its outskirts.

"It's a Uni town, supposed to get a bit lively at night," he says, all animated. "And out around here is a big wine producing region."

"Sounds ripper. So, why the fuck are we going to a snake farm?" I ask, mock-testily. "We've got plenty of snakes in Australia."

"Even in Sydney?"

"One or two," I say.

We've got snakes in Sydney, alright. They slither across the dancefloor in Three Wise Monkeys, wrapping themselves around women, looking for one who'll milk their venom. That's where I met Neville. In Australia we say that the only good snake is a dead one.

"But I'm sure you've got students and wine there too."

"Fair one. How do you know all this stuff anyway, Dan?"

"I read about it."

Ah. So that's how people find out about stuff. I'm not much of a reader. Back in our…back in *my* flat, I've even got magazines with bookmarks in them. I like getting emails, though.

The snake farm's a pretty interesting place, actually. Not quite as enthralling as Dan seems to find it, though. I lose him again, even though he's right next to me. He insists on reading each of those little cards in the corner of the tanks. Who reads those? Seriously. But it's nice to have someone next to me. Men are like radiators: good to cosy up against, bad to be handcuffed to. Thankfully, there's no tour guide today, whose arse Dan can completely disappear up.

It's all going well, until we get to the tank with the articulated python. I might have got that name wrong. It's sleeping soundly on a tree cutting, but lying on the sawdust in front of it are three dead chicks. All in a row like an Easter decoration for sickos.

"Why would it do that?" I ask Dan. "Kill them and just leave them there? That's so horrible."

Teach me, O Wise Master. Help me to understand.

"Dunno," he replies. "Maybe it likes cold cuts."

He's a smartarse, but at least I finally asked a question he doesn't know the answer to. I hear a noise that sounds like someone's watch alarm going off and look around. There's no one else here, but it seems really close. Then I see it: right at the very front of the python's tank. One little chick, still alive and chirping.

Jesus Christ. All this horror and I haven't even made it out into the jungle yet. Next year I'll go to Disneyland, ride the teacups all day long. I point it out to Dan.

"That's not good," he says, stating the blindingly obvious.

"Just doesn't seem right," I reply, holding my hand up to the glass and then retracting it hastily as the chick begins to move toward it.

"Maybe we could buy it out. Like a field negro, or a Bangkok bargirl."

"Going cheep," I say, a bit cheaply. "But what would we do with it?"

"We'd raise it like our own. Get it into a good school. Let it make its own decisions about religion and drugs and sexuality. Love it and support it, whatever it decides to do. And it'd still end up hating us."

So, we're a "we" now. I think he intended that last remark to cheer me up. I think I'm supposed to be laughing. I start crying instead. Dan looks surprised, puts his arm around me, says nothing. I lean in close to him, cleaning his dirty T-shirt with my tears. I find myself suddenly wishing the streets of Stellenbosch were lined with fluffy little corpses, if that's what it takes to have him near to me.

Dan: My Grandmother and Other Dead Relatives

She came to the funeral. I fully expected that she would, unable to resist the glue of free grief to sniff up. Midway through the sparsely attended service, she slithered into the back row of the church like a humbled demon. She sat an expectedly safe distance away from the font; far from the splash zone.

I was sat next to one of the twins, Esther I think. She didn't know my Grandma, but had come to show her support.

"My sister sends her regards," she whispered. "She doesn't do funerals. She lost her only child when she was very young. She hasn't been very good at coping with death since. Or life, really."

"How long ago was that?" I asked.

"Fifty four years ago," she replied, flicking invisible dust from her dress. "People always say that things get better with time. They don't. They just get older, like everything else. Like the people who say that."

As much as I admired her candour, I couldn't help but feel that her timing was a little off.

"If you're here; she's here," I offered. It was the best I could do at short notice.

She laid her hand on my sleeve throughout the service, only removing it to rub her desecrated temple. Tuning herself in, picking up progress reports from her sister, back running the shop on her own. I could feel her steady pulse on my forearm throughout the service and was reminded of snorkelling in Hanuma Bay, Hawaii, a giant turtle swimming alongside me for a time, its wizened flipper slowly beating against the back of my leg. I thought of this woman here with me then and I loved her, whoever she was.

I didn't even know my mother was there, until she saw fit to draw my attention with some overly theatrical sobs that came vaulting over a pew.

I knew it would be her, but I didn't so much as turn around to look at her. It was a day designed to mark someone's absence, not recognise another's unwanted presence. She collared me outside the church after the service.

"Can I have a word?" she asked.

This is customary, a standard opener for social workers or the police. Sometimes they even arrive together.

It's never good news.

Certainly, you can have a word. How about "abandonment"? How about "neglect"? How about "murderess"? How about "abandoning, neglectful, murderous bitch"? Admittedly, that was more than one word, and still more sprang to mind, but none of them came from my lips. As it was, I just nodded curtly, and glared down upon her as the gargoyles did.

She is my mother, after all.

I looked over to the church gate to see my Grandma's friend Bert, viewing the two of us with some consternation. I gave him a little semaphored signal of acquiescence, went to hand him my house keys, motioned for the funeral party to follow him. They tottered away cautiously on canes and frames, back to her nearby house. Our house. My house. My own walk back to where my mother was stood was no quicker or less painful.

Annoyingly, she looked quite good. Good being a relative concept as far as my mother is concerned. Good meaning she didn't look like she'd flown in on a crop duster. Good meaning that her make-up wasn't circumnavigating her own face. Good meaning that she was sober. Both her hand and gaze were steady, I could tell she hadn't taken a drink for a while. She looked a hell of a lot better than the last time I saw....

"When was the last time I saw you?" she asked, all casual, as though we were two old friends who'd just met unexpectedly by the supermarket's reduced shelf.

Oh, I remembered the last time I saw her…

Dan: Immodesty Baize

I was seventeen years old and working a Youth Training Scheme in a plumbing supplies warehouse on the outskirts of Doncaster. Friday Flyer, early finish. Me and two other apprentices, Tommy and Hywel, caught the Little Nipper bus into town. We made a beeline for The Railway Tavern, a rundown old pub with a half blind landlord, known for its tolerance of underage drinkers.

Hywel was the youngest and the smallest, shorter than any sentence I could use to describe him. As such, it was his practice to head to the bar first, confront the issue head on, brazen it out rather than skulking sheepishly behind us bigger lads looking guilty. Not that it made much difference in The Railway, where the fat, gamey old landlord would top a gripe water bottle up with vodka if you so desired it.

Something caught his attention in the backroom and he paused on the way.

"Heyup, Roberts!" he cried. "Looks like your mam's in!"

I turned to see her, asleep on the pool table at two o'clock in the afternoon. She was snoring lightly, an eyebrow twitching intermittently. One shoe fallen to the floor, next to a deserted and upturned raffia shopping bag full of bottles. A lone tin of Tesco Value soup had made an abortive roll for freedom and now nestled undetected under a corner pocket. Mulligatawny. Bangs of lank hair smashing into her silica gel mouth.

Hywel didn't know. He was from the other side of Doncaster. The marginally better side. We had only met through work. He had meant it as a joke. But Tommy knew; he and I had grown up together. I looked from the prone form on the table to him. His face burned post box red, to offset the gangrenous tint of mine.

A group of Council workers in hi-vis vests were huddled around the fruit machine in the backroom. One of their number was returning from the toilet, still packing himself away. You could peg him as the jester of the group all too easily, a belled hat traded in for a back-to-front baseball cap, a paint-spattered crude slogan on his T-shirt. One who would sport a Disney Store tie for a day at the races. As he passed the pool table, he deftly flicked the hem of her crumpled skirt up the back, laughing and mock-running to the safety of his crew, who had obviously dared him to do it.

He didn't need to run. She slept right through it.

Mission accomplished. He had successfully humiliated an alcoholic. Bravo, sir. The other men greeted him like he had just shot a tiger. But their uproarious cheers and laughter slowly died down into silence and dissolved into wistful head-shakes as they regarded her still unperturbed frame.

Someone's mother.

Not mine. Not anymore.

"View any better from your side lads?" the Joker asked, losing his audience, looking to us. Working the room now.

From their position at the other side of the table, they couldn't see what we saw. The cellulite, a slight, blueberried rash at the top of one thigh. Gunmetal grey nylon knickers caked with spots of dried blood.

My hand instinctively closed around a heavy pint pot, my glare fixed upon the highly visible buffoon playing to the court. Tommy's mammoth hand closed on top of mine. He leaned in close and whispered:

"Let it go, Dan," he said. "It's the weekend."

We both knew all too well what he meant. Police cells are a lot noisier on a Friday night, their inhabitants drunker and angrier, their floors never any warmer. Then he turned to Hywel, raising his voice.

"This place is fucking rank," he said. "Let's get some tinnies and sit by the canal. It's nice out."

Hywel was still staring over at her, with a look of complete revulsion on his face.

"Yeah," he said limply. "*Vamos.*"

We made our way toward the door, but just before we slipped out, Tommy headed towards the backroom. Approaching the stilled life, he stopped, taking her in for a moment, with an embalmer's appraising eye. With the kind of startling grace that big people often possess, he gently removed the dream-catching strand of hair from her mouth and brushed it back against her cheek.

I remembered then how light and fine her hair had once been. Chestnut strands of it falling through my shrivelled fingers like ambitions as she carried me down the stairs, after bath time, when I was a small child. I was swaddled in warm towels, drawn from my favourite hiding place. The airing cupboard, rumbling heart of the house. Dried gently in front of the living room's gas fire.

Arms up, little soldier.

That done, Tommy smoothed her skirt down and fixed the labourers with a threatening stare that shouted:

Leave.

Well.

Alone.

He was a big lad for his age, butting past the six foot barrier even then, and slowly growing just as wide through a steady diet of Spar Pick n' Mix and sparring with pricks and Micks. His sweet tooth contrasted sharply with a sour disposition directed toward anyone who got on the wrong side of him. He was maybe the one seventeen-year-old in the world at that time who could stare down a saloon full of navvies. Joker returned to his friends, and their chastened gazes dipped first to their shoes and then back to the bandit's mesmeric light and noise. The fat man seated behind the bar, however, watched these events with interest over the top of his half-moon glasses.

"Do you know her?" he barked, even his voice fat. "Cos I've got a pool tournament tonight and she's slavering all over me fucking baize."

"Nah," I called out, already halfway through the swing door. "We don't know her."

Dan: Crappy Expectations

Back in the graveyard, I still didn't know her, and she was still waiting for an answer to her question.

"Dunno," I said, eloquently.

"She was a good woman, your Grandma."

"You didn't kill her, did you?" I replied, only half kidding. I wouldn't put total obliteration of our bloodline past my mother.

"Well, what a thing to say!" she exclaimed. Indignation didn't suit her as well as black did. With a now standardized lack of decorum, she reeled back, seating herself on a gravestone. Just as abruptly, she realised what she had done and pitched forward again, wiping herself hurriedly. As though she could catch her death. Smoothing down her own skirt now, I noted, a walking model of rehabilitation. Struggling to recover her poise, she fumbled in her bag for cigarettes, before realising that too was a no-no. She made one of those facial gestures that in a comic-book would have a thought bubble saying "harrumph" above it.

"What were you doing going to see her in the home?" I asked.

"I...used to look in on her from time to time, mostly while you were away," she said. She still had the cigarette in her hand, drew it up to her mouth at one point before stopping herself. She gave a rueful little chuckle, like a child molester's afterthought. "You almost caught me once, getting back off your last trip."

Freshly cut flowers in my Grandma's room. I got back from Africa early, moved my flight forward a couple of days. I did it because I couldn't face being alone after those days with Amber in Cape Town. The nurses weren't expecting me. I remembered the startled receptionist on my first returning visit, eyes darting from me to the carpark behind.

"Why would you do that?" I asked.

"Someone had to," she said.

I could have done with a cigarette myself at that point. The old cow still had a few moves on her, still knew just the requisite amount of force needed to drive a sharpened HB pencil right into your Achilles heel. Not so deft with the backtracking though:

"I think it's really great, Dan, all the places you've been. It's more than most folk round here do," she said, unconvincingly. She sounded all wrong then, a hyena modulating its pitch to cough up a miaow. "Your dad would've..."

"Would've what?" I interjected, and she said nothing.

"WOULD'VE WHAT?" I repeated, in capitals this time.

She said nothing.

"If you can't finish your sentence we can go ask him," I said levelly, gesturing across the churchyard. "He's just over there, spinning quite rapidly now probably."

Finishing his own sentence, in a plot that she ghost wrote.

"What's that supposed to mean?" she asked, and when I said nothing she sighed and started walking over towards a nearby bench, fumbling for her cigarettes again already.

"I think we need to talk," she said, from there. The cheap click of a Clipper lighter a cheap trick of diversion. In spite of my every bio-rhythm ebbing in the opposite direction on hearing that all too woefully familiar phrase, I found myself following in her wake sleepily.

Once there, I sat at the same distance someone might sit from a man wearing a beard made of bees. I saw myself from above, listening to everything she had to say, passing no comment throughout. A bronze statue of a seated figure on a graveyard bench. My mother, the tourist, next to him, blowing cigarette smoke and innuendo in his hardened and immobile face.

When she seemed to have finished, when I could take no more, I stood and walked away from her, without pausing to look in her direction.

"All this anger, Dan," she called to the irate, wakening hairs on the back of my neck. "You need to let it go."

She didn't come to the reception. She wasn't invited. By the time I got there, the small, attendant crowd were situated comfortably in the house. The Old Sailor Bert had marshalled them well, navigated them towards the port. And the sherry. His young wife, my Grandma's friend Cassie, mutinied on him many years ago, leaving him all at sea. She grew lonely while he was away, during one of those long Northern winters where the days are really just nights you have to live through. Except that she couldn't. She sat out on a deckchair in the backyard one evening and emptied her wrists onto the tarmac, not wishing to mess up the house. I wouldn't be so churlish as to suggest that Bert never looked at another woman for the rest of his life, but I'm certain every time he did it was Cassie's face he saw first.

He shook my hand for the fourth time that day, with the same over-firm shake favoured by rugby players and Long Island industrialists. I regarded his still brawny arms. Saw the naval tattoos, inky tachometers of his travel that had so bewitched me as a child, straining through his cheap, white shirt.

"Alright, lad?" he asked.

"Yep," I replied.

That's how Yorkshire men open up to each other.

"She asked after you the last time I went to see her, y'know," he offered.

"Did she?" I asked, prizing him open to reveal this pearl. "What did she say?"

"She asked if you'd painted that front door yet."

"Oh," I said. More of a winkle than an oyster, then. "I haven't."

"So I can see. Listen, I could do it if you…"

"No," I interjected, too firmly. "*I'll* do it."

"Right you are."

We both turned then, daftly looking in the direction of the obscured front door for a long moment.

"Maybe not now, though, eh?"

"No, lad," said Bert, smiling. "Probably not now. Guests and that."

Bert was my best friend there then, fifty years my senior, and yet I still found myself wondering if I could beat him in a fight. He had brought radishes from his allotment, for some reason I couldn't entirely fathom. I received them with a dull nod of non-comprehension, still processing the information I had received from my mother in the graveyard. Molly from two doors down had brought a fruitcake. Some brought fastidious smiles. Others, I didn't even know. Obituary hawks, scanning The Green Paper every week, looking for some reason to dust down their wide-brimmed hats and polish up their patent leather shoes.

Everyone spoke very highly of her, everyone was polite and respectful. But I couldn't help thinking that there were elderly people in my Grandma's house that weren't my Grandma, and that she wouldn't set foot here or anywhere else ever again. A downbeat masquerade ball.

Upstairs, in a bedroom drawer, I sensed my passport humming into life, its worn pages flicking back and forth restlessly, like it was some enchanted spell-book.

I re-boiled the kettle so many times that it began whistling in anguish. Two nurses from the home arrived, looking strangely amiss in black outfits with no upside-down watches pinned to their breast pockets. I approached them with the notion of speaking to them about my mother's visits to their workplace. But, halfway there, I decided that I didn't want to consider her or what she had told me anymore. Not on that day.

When I closed in, I noticed that the younger of the two was crying all the tears I hadn't yet been able to muster. Not overly given to tactility, I awkwardly gave her arm what I hoped was a reassuring squeeze. A slight misjudgement of force, and all I succeeded in doing was making her jump. After her splashdown, we exchanged platitudes like flapjack recipes for a while, before the older lady leaned in closer.

"Can I ask you a question?" she enquired.

Every time someone asks that, it always means it's something you don't want to hear. But it had been a day for that. I nodded reluctantly.

"Why have you put radishes in the fruit bowl?" she asked.

Let it go, my mother said. Fine advice to give to a pallbearer! Fine advice coming from a woman who probably only prised her chipped varnish talons from a bottle of Buckfast a couple of months ago! But it wasn't even my mother speaking. Just a few words from her sponsor, whoever's goodwill she was now leeching from.

I am not my mother's son, and I will not fall for her lies. She was little more than the leaky vessel that bore me for nine months and tossed me overboard for twenty some years. I am the grandson of Lucy Roberts, whose body I interred, whose long life was the epitome of perseverance. The heart of a lion, beating through the ribcage of a sparrow. A caring woman whose delicate fingers moulded bullets that strafed the bodies of Nazis. I am the son of Alfie Roberts, whose body I also interred, who descended into hell every night to put fish fingers on my plate. A father who went down fighting, spitting tarred sputum into the face of an uncaring God. I am the by-product of a dozen broken foster homes, homes that I mostly broke. I am the square peg forced into the round hole of the system. I didn't fit. I smashed the system. I am a killer of magpies. I am a warrior, blooded in a hundred street fights across the world. Maybe not a hundred, and I probably lost more than I won. But my grip will neither weaken nor falter. I am the spirit of our dog Sabre incarnate, a bullish terrier ragging, ragging, ragging away at life.

I will never let it go.

Amber: Go Fish

"You look beautiful," says Dan.

"Thanks."

It sounds really big-headed to say this, but I actually know that I do. It took me two hours to get there, though. Two hours doing my make-up in front of a grubby little mirror in the dorm room, while a Melbournite coming down off magic mushrooms lay on her bed calling out Kenny Rogers's name and pressing my dress under the mattress.

Dan told me I could get ready in his en-suite but I wanted to surprise him. He looks nice, too, although his shirt seems like it's been ironed with a house-brick and his usually messy hair might have been slicked down with margarine. I'm almost tempted to roll a breadstick around in it.

We're sat in a fancy restaurant for our last supper. I'm about to order pasta but Dan, font of all knowledge, insists that I should try the seafood while I'm here in Cape Town.

"I don't generally eat seafood, though. Except for spaghetti carbonara."

"But you live by the sea," says Dan, frowning.

"Yeah," I say. "But it's not like they make it compulsory or anything."

"It goes well with white wine."

"Okay, I'll try it," I reply. He knows the way to an Australian girl's heart: straight through her kidneys, just like Lozzer says.

As usual, he's right. I don't mean about me living by the sea; obviously I was aware of that. About the food. The smug bastard. We order a big platter of all different kinds of fish and everything tastes amazing. When we're done, the table is like the inside of a whale, littered with fish bones and shrimp tails and lobster shells. We sit back, exhausted and content. If I wasn't all dolled up I'd love to do a big clearance burp. But there's just one thing missing.

"I can't see my snatch!" I suddenly blurt out.

"It was quite a big meal," says Dan, laughing.

"It's not funny, Dan! Where's my snatch?" I ask, more frantically, bobbing my head around.

"Try to think of the last place you saw it," he says. He's looking puzzled now, but he's still laughing. I've no idea why. I ignore him, duck my head under the table and then I see it. It's slid off my chair and has fallen down between my feet. I plonk it up on the table and pull my ciggies out of it angrily. He's still fucking laughing.

"What's so funny?"

"I think the word you were looking for is *clutch*," he says, pointing over to my spangly little bag. "Not snatch."

"Oh," I say, exhaling smoke, reddening as I finally catch on.

"You do tickle me, Amber."

"Glad to hear it," I say, still a bit narked about him laughing at me. "When I first met you I thought your head was gonna explode if you cracked a smile."

"And now what do you think?"

"You're alright," I say, giving him a playful little kick under the table. "Do you like me?"

"I love you," he says.

"I love you too," I say, without thinking. Then I think I've ballsed up again, because it sounded like he said it with a little 'l' and I just said it with a big 'L.'

Now it's quiet. Now we're both looking at each other in a *which-one-of-us-just-farted* kind of way. Now we're both glancing around the restaurant, looking for an old guy or a dog to blame it on. Now we look like two open goalposts at opposing ends of a footie field. And there aren't any bones on the table anymore, just a two-ton elephant squatting on the centre half line.

It's the first one I've seen in Africa so far.

I know that it'll be me who has to speak first, because otherwise Dan will slip into one of his *petit-mal* trances. Big shout out to the Associated Health Board of New South Wales for making me sit through that child psychology primer! It's really helped me understand how men think.

"Well," I say, summing everything up.

"Yep," says Dan.

"Now what?"

"Dessert, maybe?" he says, fanning himself with a menu, turning burgundy like its cover.

"You do know that I'm leaving tomorrow, don't you?"

"Course I do."

"It's gone fast, don't you think?"

"Everything goes fast when you're around, Amber. That's why I like you being around."

"How do you feel about me leaving?"

"I don't want you to go."

"Maybe I'll stay, then."

"You should go, though. I don't want you to, but you have to. You really need to see Africa. It's amazing."

"I know that I should," I say. "But maybe if you tied me to your bed I wouldn't be able to."

"Didn't we do that already?" he asks.

We did. But there's no wiggle room this time, not after this conversation. And there are no more safety words, not now. Fuck it, I'll just...

"I'll only be on the trip for three weeks," I say, my voice trembling. "You could come to Sydney after that. You could stay...you could stay with me. You could stay with me for as long as you wanted to."

He doesn't say anything for ages and I know that means he's going to say no. And I'm an idiot. I've hung myself out to dry again and now I'm flapping in the wind. I only met him at that hostel bar a few days ago and it would have been so easy to leave him alone. And he seemed like the kind of guy who would have been quite happy to be left alone. But I just couldn't do it, because I didn't want to be alone, not even for a second.

Because in spite of all my new so-called empowerment, I only really booked onto this trip so I wouldn't be alone. And it hasn't even started yet but I'm already dreading the day it's over and I have to go back to my empty flat. I'll hang my coat on that stupid chair just inside the doorway like I always do and it'll slip to the ground like it always does and the only person who'll ever pick it up again will be me.

"Okay," he says, smiling. "I'll see you there."

And I feel happy and dizzy and I want to kiss him. Then I realise that would be quite an appropriate thing to do in this moment! So I lean forward across the table and put my greasy mouth on his. The elephant is gone now and I can feel fish bones and shrimp tails and lobster shells squishing under my hands, like I'm tramping down on all the skeletons of the past as I move forward into tomorrow.

Dan: Where There's a Will

When the sun sneaks up to the kitchen window like a strung-out thief, I might catch a latent fingerprint on the bread bin. Or on the now abandoned teapot, still gleaming on the outside, blackened like a cancerous bowel on the inside. Accessories after the fact of her, trace elements brought to the kitchen table.

Me? I am the fungus spore under the fridge light. All that I grew from is taken away from me, or expires before me. I alone remain, undetected, spoiling everything.

The house feels louder and smaller with her gone. This is odd, as she hadn't entered the premises in over a year. By night, the timbers creak in despair. The noise abates, the walls close in, the building settles for me.

The house misses her, as do I. She bought it outright from the council many years ago, just as she once tried to barter me back from them. I own it now. I am finally laird to the estate but, just like her, I'm not there.

My Grandma also bequeathed me a modest sum of money, and I have unwisely chosen to invest it in my past.

I still have one last magpie to step on.

20th September 2016

From: danroberts@h–mail.com

To: tommylayspipe@whizzymail.com.au

RE: Sydney

I'm heading over your way in a few weeks. Fancy meeting up?

21st September 2016

From: tommylayspipe@whizzymail.com.au

To: danroberts@h-mail.com

RE: Sydney

What did you do this time?

INCIDENT REPORT
COMPLAINANT: Dan Roberts
LOCATION: Doncaster, England

"You're suffocating me," she said. At least, I think that's what she said. Her words came out fast and garbled when I popped a breathing hole in the plastic bag.

Kidding.

"There's this guy at work," that's what she said. That's how she began. That's how we ended. A slow death in the living room of our small flat, with the end credits rolling on a DVD and a scrapyard of Chinese takeaway cartons cluttering the coffee table. Julie. My ex-girlfriend. She went on, like they always do. "We haven't *done* anything. But...I *like* him."

I said nothing. Sat Tonto, heap faithful understudy about to saddle up and become The Lone Ranger. Angered by my silence, she delivered the rest of her story as laboriously as possible. Like a forceps birth.

"He's smart...and he's funny...and he's kind. He's going places. I don't think you're going anywhere. I don't think we're going anywhere."

That struck me as paradoxical when she was the one who had wanted a quiet night in. But now I knew why. I tried to visualise this man, this man that turned her head as he strolled through Human Resources like a fucking prince. I wondered if he was handsome. I wondered if his ears were burning.

"Are you going to say anything at all, Dan?"

"Go," I said.

I stood up too quickly, experienced that fleeting moment of inertia that happens when you first set foot on an escalator. I walked over to the flat's door and punched a hole right through the cheap wood, to illustrate the preferred route for her departure. Had I stayed she might have left via the window.

I went straight to the one place around here where people go when they choose to bungee jump away from their own life. The Railway Tavern. The last place I saw my mother. The last place I took a drink. The last place on earth.

I selected gin, which is known for restoring pep in the drinker. I wanted to abort all my memories of her, piss them out like kidney stones in the morning. During the night, even, in our bed. In my bed. Who would complain now?

Several hours later, I raised my head again, finally awoken from brief slumber when my own drool traversed the uneven surface of the bar and arrived at my eye. A familial trait. I woke up gristly and liverish, a fat landlord and an old man with a dog staring over at me.

"Problem?" I asked.

"No problem, son," said the landlord, wearily. "Sights like you are why I wanted to get into this game in the first place."

"I'm not your son. I'm not anybody's son. I'm not anybody's anything anymore. And I want another fucking drink."

"I'd recommend you go elsewhere, then," he replied. "I'm not serving yer anymore."

I appraised the three of them through one eye. The landlord: too fat to fight. The best way to defeat him would have been to puncture him. The old boy: blow a raspberry in his ear trumpet and he'd probably keel over. The dog: possibly more game, but I like dogs. Julie and me were going to get a dog. I stood up and made to leave, then turned in the doorway.

"Listen," I said. Then I forgot what I was going to say and left.

I fared no better in the pizza place, sliding down a plastic chair and goading the proprietor:

"Italians used to own this place," I slurred. From my low vantage point I couldn't even see him, and so directed my vitriol towards a charity box shaped like a blind boy. "You'd come in 'ere, order a pizza and watch 'em flipping the dough and chopping the peppers. Now it's all frozen bases and toppings out of Tupperware."

The owner's head popped up to see what I was rambling on about.

"An' there used to be a big fuck off clay oven right where you're leaning," I added.

He wasn't leaning. My eyes were.

"Smokeless zone now though, innit boss?" he replied, shrugging.

There was little I could say or do to offend him. A Turkish émigré, he was subjected to nightly jibes concerning camel racing and ham-and-pineapple fisted diatribes about Muslim extremism from white men acting like little pink boys. Showing off in front of their mates and showing their arses to the girls walking past the window. When he answered his daily calls to prayer the greatest pleasure facing towards Mecca gave him was that it meant he could turn his back on everything here.

I was trying to make a point about people leaving and he just wanted me to leave.

I left. Bounced off walls and shop fronts, cradling the pizza like a baby, a cheesy umbilical cord already stretched between the box and my mouth. One of the streetlamps I bumped into had a date. A young vagrant, with a tea-cosy hat and skin resembling the inside of the pot.

"Spare any change, mate?" he asked. "It's cold out here. Can't get no shuteye."

As though small change would help that. As though he might insulate himself with copper. I considered that he might have a better chance of sleeping if he wasn't bedding down under a streetlamp. I knew I didn't have any money left because I'd just sprayed the rest of my shrapnel at a Turk. I passed him a slice of pizza. He took it and sniffed at it as though I were proffering a shoe.

"What good is that to me?" he asked.

What did he want me to do? Bring tofu and a five-bean salad?

"They don't make 'em with heroin on, son," I replied.

He threw the slice at my face. It hit me triangular on the forehead, then slid down my nose and flopped over like a fortune-telling fish, right back into the vaginal section of the box I had birthed it from.

Then I dropped the box to the ground.

Then I dropped him to the ground.

I don't know how long I was hitting him for, but I do know that after a while his face started to feel malleable. Like Play-Doh. He never threw a punch, or struggled, or made a sound throughout. When I was finished I couldn't even really see a face anymore beneath all the blood and lumps. I couldn't tell if he was alive or dead. Panicked, I drew his cardboard bedding up around him. He looked like a calzone.

I was running again. I went back to the flat and packed a bag. There wasn't anything left of Julie inside. A draught had come through the hole in the door and blown everything away. The dressing table undressed without all those balms and potions. The drawers she kept her clothes in poking out like tongues. I put my hand inside one of them, stroked the wallpaper that lined it, wondered who would go to such trouble to provide decor for inanimate objects. Then I closed it firmly.

My Grandma still lived alone then. I used my house-key, left a note stuck to the fridge with saliva I could barely produce. I told her that I'd gone to find myself, when the exact opposite was true. I took the first train to London in the morning and gave all the coins in my pocket to a homeless lady there, tears in my eyes as I did so. I caught a flight to Australia two days later. Where all the English criminals used to go.

It was my first big trip overseas. Tommy was waiting for me at Sydney airport, like I know he always will be. He was smiling at first, because I hadn't told him why I was coming. I stayed in Australia for five months, until the fruit-picking season ended and the money ran out.

I never did learn the fate of the homeless man. People can disappear so easily.

When I came back to England, I expected to be arrested as soon as the plane landed in Heathrow. I was both relieved and disappointed when I wasn't.

22nd September 2016

From: danroberts@h-mail.com

To: amonsafari@whizzymail.com.au

RE: Closure

Dear Amber,

I'd like to apologise for some of the ideas expressed in these previous messages. Don't we all have things we'd like to take back? Certain recent events in my home life have caused me to re-evaluate matters. More than anything now, I'd like to draw this problem between us to a close, as quickly as possible.

It's all too easy to get dragged down in the quick-sands of time. Clocks whizz around like Catherine wheels and lives are Chinese sky lanterns that splutter out in the dark night. No matter what may have happened between us since (not much, admittedly), we were very close once, Amber. It saddens me to think we'll never speak again. However, for us at least, there is still time.

If you won't expedite the closure of this matter between us then I will. For reasons that I won't detail here, I recently came into a modest amount of money. I used it to purchase a flight.

How are things in Sydney these days? Can you still order a five-dollar steak? Probably not. Will there be a fireworks display over the harbour bridge this evening? I expect it's likely – they always seem to find some reason for a fireworks display there. The dogs of Sydney must live in a perpetual state of fear, with suspected terror level colour-charts posted up inside their kennels. Except dogs have difficulty differentiating between colours so, considering their dichromatic impunity, they would be much better served with a numerical system.

Heathrow to Sydney. Twenty-five hours is a long time in the air, but I can easily lose a day if it means I get my life back. And my money.

Be seeing you, Amber.

Dan.

Dan: Off the Rails

No more emails. I fired a warning shot across the world just to be sporting, but we're into Black Ops territory now. I can't have Amber knowing my exact whereabouts. I wouldn't want to spoil the surprise.

Coming in, weapons hot.

The train from my hometown passed directly through Doncaster without stopping, which is always a wise policy. In the run up to the station, stands a former engineering works, long since closed. There's a rust scabbed sign I notice in the carpark every time the train passes it:

MUSTER POINT!

Exclamation mark, model's own. A fire drill assembly point, clearly. I've always liked that sign, and never seen or heard the phrase used anywhere else. Today it felt fitting, as I headed out past it and toward my own.

I'm back in Sheffield, again. I have to catch an early National Express bus to Heathrow tomorrow, but for the moment, I'm feeling secondary at the Premier Inn, the same place where I once brushed up on my Slovenian. And I still can't open the shampoo sachet. I'm really more comfortable in the surrounds of hostels but, in these parts, hostels are a different proposition entirely. They have sharps bins in the toilets and you sleep with your wallet under your pillow. You leave it in your trousers, just in case the other residents steal those too. Although, maybe I should have done that in Cape Town.

I think about how I'm heading down, just like my Grandma. She never flew anywhere in her life. Some people don't like even the notion of it, but I love it. I went to Krakow once and all the Poles on the plane clapped as we landed.

What peasants, I thought.

This harsh perspective of mine was no doubt influenced by the fact that one strange man, with a face carved out of corned beef and a side order of congealed spaghetti hoops affixed to his jacket, was caught smoking in the toilets *before* take-off. Also, I imagined their reaction to be tempered by the fact that we were flying no-frills with EasyJet, and as such were lucky to have touched down in one piece at all.

But, looking at it now, the Poles have got the right idea.

We *should* applaud. We should award sainthoods to Louis Bleriot, The Wright Brothers, Amelia Earhart, Charles Lindbergh...anyone at all who expedited this amazing process, all the way up to and excluding Richard Branson. Flying is an everyday miracle that we all take for granted. The fact that all those big winged Pringle containers seated on the runway can actually take off and land safely. The fact that you can cross a body of water as vast as the Atlantic in six hours. We're all birds now. Time flies, but so do we.

Dan: Tommy

So, here I am.

I exited the baggage carousel area at Sydney Airport and the woman at Immigration Control stamped my passport like she was committing a hate crime.

"You know you can't win, don'tcha?" she spat.

"What?" I replied, startled.

"The Ashes, mate," she said, suddenly beaming.

At those words, I flashed first on my Grandmother, then Amber. My brain hijacked by bandits during the flight, my thoughts like rusted coins jamming in their slots. I'd forgotten how devastatingly witty Australians are. Passing through the sliding doors to the other side of the world, the first face I saw was an old one from my exit point. It was Tommy's enormous belfry, eclipsing all others, blotting out the sun. He was towering above the taxi drivers (who tend to be rendered small and wide, compressed and canned) in Arrivals. I briefly wondered why they were all staring at me like I was vomit on a communion dress, until I saw he was holding up a handmade sign that said:

A Pederast.

Another funny fucker.

"Danny Boy," he declared. "Man on a Mission. Missionary Man. Missionary Dan."

He had been pre-briefed.

And he talks like that.

You get used to it.

He was fatter than I remembered, but then we all are now. Other than that, he looked to be in crude health, even incorporating his inflated adjustments. Gone South. Gone soft. Less clenched, much more at home in his own tanned skin now that he was far from there. He gave me a gristly bear hug and a slap on the back that bruised my inner child.

"When was the last time I saw you?" he asked.

When was the last time someone asked me that question? Mother Magwitch, in the graveyard. The baggage carousel goes round and round, a snake belt cinched at the waist of the world, indenting on its tired skin, crushing ice caps, sinking Venice.

Best not to use the word "carousel" in front of Tommy though, for reasons I'll explain later.

"Dunno," I said.

"Sorry to hear about your, er..." he faltered.

Grandma, I thought. The word is Grandma. Other people may still need that name, even if I don't. It shouldn't go into the earth with her. After that, I exchanged money and some gruff banter, carefully tailored to conccal any suggestion of inter-male tenderness. Then, all caught up, we drove back to Tommy's home in the Surry Hills district of Sydney.

Albion Street, of all places.

"Full of poofs, round here," he said, parking his van, shrugging. "Nice people though. Keen recyclers."

He had made good, starting as a plumber's apprentice, working and crawling his way up through the S-bends, owning his own business now. Done it the right way, by keeping his large head down, tucking it under sinks that water flows down the wrong way.

"Brits do well here," he explained, too loud, still on the street, fumbling for house keys. "No work ethic, yer Aussies. First bit of sun and they're calling in sick, off down the beach. First bit of rain and they're calling in sick, won't walk through puddles in their flip-flops. You want an Aussie plumber, you have to Google a five-day weather forecast and book him for a temperate day. Just hope the Poles never make it over here. If they do then we're all fucked. No EasyJet flights to Sydney yet, though, eh? Did you fetch me them Toblerones?"

We entered the living room and the first thing I saw on the mantelpiece was a picture of him with his girlfriend. She was very pretty, but looked petite enough to fit easily inside his mouth.

"She around?" I asked.

"Nah," he said with a shrug. "Gone walkabout. She reckoned she had to go away to find herself. I haven't got a clue where she is now."

He traced a finger along the glass tenderly, then drew it back and dead-armed her image in the face. It sent the picture-frame smashing back into the mantle, before careening down the floor. He raked over the broken glass with a worryingly exposed flip-flopped foot.

"Lasses, eh?" he said, distractedly.

"Nothing but trouble," I offered.

He gave me the short tour of his modest - but well furnished - home. Pointed out the specifications of the plasma TV and the surround sound system, even beseeching me to admire the smooth, automated motion of the electronic blinds in his window, worked by a remote control. I didn't know that such things existed. I watched not them, but my oldest friend, saw the rapturous delight that a piece of material moving along a rail could engender in him. Eight o'clock in the evening and the sun still shone brazenly, as an affront to the night. The sliding blinds exposed it again and again and again, making those giddy little light bulb filaments jig around in my raw eyes, watery and blinking as tractor beams of dust particles headed toward them.

"Please stop doing that," I said.

"Bit frazzled, eh, mate? Bit tetchy? Get up on the wrong side of the world this morning, did you?" he asked, resetting the control in its holder. "I've got summat that'll smarten you right up. Wait 'til you get a load of this."

Dan: Fairground Monsters

Too tired to venture out, we instead sat out in his back yard, Tommy drinking beer and producing a hash pipe. I was surprised to see him with it. *Beatnik baccy*, I remembered him once calling it disdainfully, as he coerced a wrap of speed into his pint to fizzle away like an anti-Alka-Seltzer.

It had been so long since I indulged that I could barely remember which end to light. Instantly, I could feel the smoke rising up into my head, like the way it spreads lasciviously across nursery ceilings in home safety adverts. Smoke Kills. But that's what I needed then, something to smother the scratchy sensation in my brain and behind my eyes.

I was reminded of my last time in Australia, a stay in an artsy hostel in Byron Bay. Open mic night, earnest female singer-songwriters with stickers on their guitars. Jenny wrens warbling odes of commitment-phobic boyfriends and menstrual cramps. Their anguished voices cracking through the marijuana haze like the muffled screams of selkies being harpooned by rummed-up sailors in the fog.

At the stroke of midnight, an Aboriginal Seer gathered us in a circle, to cast out our bad spirits with a tea tray full of smouldering eucalyptus leaves. His young nephew accompanied him and, earlier at the bar, he had told me that his uncle was also a shape-shifter, who could take on the form of any indigenous creature.

"I doubt he'll do it tonight though," he said, deadpan. "Too hard to hold the tray."

When the smoking leaves were proffered under my nose, the Seer regarded me studiously as I inhaled. Nodding sagely, he moved onto the next participant, then stopped, doubled back and offered them up to me again.

"I think you need another go around, mate," he said.

My reverie broke like a fever as an elbow slipped off the arm of the lawn chair, erroneously supplanted on concrete. I watched it hanging there languidly for a good long time before a tugging sensation in my upper torso reminded me it was mine. My head turned with the smooth, automated slide of Tommy's blinds. I saw him suppressing giggles.

"Been a while, eh?" he asked, and I wasn't sure if he was talking about the pot, or the proximity.

"Oof," I replied.

He was still staring at me, appraising me as the Seer had. I didn't like it, never have liked people looking at me.

"What the fuck are you looking at?" I enquired, my voice set at a lower speed now.

"Can't say, mate," he replied. "I haven't got me monster book with me."

We laughed for a long time at that soured old joke from our past, until it reminded me of another one.

"D'you remember that afternoon in The Railway Tavern?" I asked. "That little style makeover you gave my…"

Now there was a word I couldn't say. I let its absence hang there between us like my arm had. He shifted awkwardly in his plastic chair, as people are wont to do often in plastic chairs. Advantage regained, I reclined further back in mine, drawing comfort from his lack of it. Saw folds of his fat trying to escape through the slats at the rear of his seat. Split sausages in a frying pan.

"I do," he said, eventually. "I mean, she was in a state alright, but she was still your mam. I always remember when we used to camp out in your backyard in the summer. She used to bring us choccy biscuits. I never got choccy biscuits at home."

I had forgotten about that. Tommy didn't get chocolate biscuits because Tommy didn't have a dad pulling down a good wage from the pit. As a kid, he spent whatever money he had on the sweets his mum couldn't afford to buy him. At school dinners, he would always eat his pudding first, unable to resist the siren's song of a cooling rhubarb crumble. Tommy didn't have a dad at all, at least not one that he or his mother could ever put a name to. No one to wrestle with in the garden, no one to chrome down his BMX, no one's penis to sneak furtive glances at in the swimming baths changing room on a Sunday morning.

At least, no one related.

Like many a small town lass before her, his mother fell prey to the advances of a fairground gypsy, who span her dizzyingly fast in her Coaster carriage and later plied her with cheap wine behind a generator unit. After the fair had left, when the only evidence of all those toffee apples consumed was the ensuing epidemic of gut-rot, she found her own belly swollen with child at the age of fifteen. Once all the Hook-A-Duck goldfish had died she was left also with a case of crabs so vicious she naively feared they might eat the baby.

She had to drop out of school due to the stigma of her ceased monthly stigmata and the resulting daily jibes. The World's Cervix, that's what they called her in the playground – proof that kids were just as cruel back then, if a little more cultured. She raised Tommy with the help of family and without any contribution from his father. Too proud to accept state help, she worked two jobs whilst looking after him. She was never anything but tired throughout her short life. She suffered a massive coronary outside CarCare in the town centre one morning and finally got the longest lie in, aged forty-eight. Tommy left for Australia two years later.

"I suppose the real reason I..." he faltered, calculated the impact of what he was about to say, proceeded anyway. "The real reason I did it, is because you didn't."

There followed a silence as wide and dry as Australia, only shattered when Tommy blustered out of the yard, sending his chair spinning on one leg in a balletic fashion.

"I fancy some choccy biscuits now we've been talking 'em up," he called, over his broad shoulder. "I'm off to the shop."

Knowing Tommy, he probably had a cupboard full of biscuits, not to mention the three giant Toblerones I had procured from Heathrow Duty Free. A door slammed in his house and the resulting backdraught blew open another one in my memory.

Dan: Taking the Biscuit

I remembered being ten years old, getting the A-frame tent for Christmas, the agonising wait that ensued to pitch it up in fairer weather. March that next year came mild, and Tommy and I could hold off no longer. We set it up in the back garden, my father hovering nearby expectantly, hunting us from behind his foxgloves. He was waiting for us to ask for help, probably both proud and a little bit disappointed when we didn't need to.

She did indeed bring us a plateful of biscuits in the early evening, but she came back later in the night too. There was a swishing at the front of the tent and I unzipped the door. My torch shone first upon her suede moccasins, damp patterns from the dewed grass rising up them like Rorschach tests. She was standing with her arms folded against the chill air, one hand pinching together the open neckline of an Aran cardigan. It was the eighties, try not to judge.

"I think you should come on in now, lads," she said. "It's too cold to be out here all night."

She was right. We had been lying there shivering and miserable, the dog installed between us, utilized as a tremulous hot water bottle. As soon as I unzipped the door fully, Sabre shot out and stood behind my mother's legs in an act of complicity. So much for that breed's supposed intransigence.

"We're alright," I said, and, in spite of her protestations, fervently maintained that line until she reluctantly went away again.

Sent back to her box, just like the dog.

An hour later, Tommy had to go out for a slash. He saw her silhouetted figure still looking out upon us from the bedroom window, an old ghost in a new story, suddenly flitting from view as he glanced in her direction.

My memories of my mother have always been selective. I remembered how the drinking started immediately after my father's death. She practically popped a bottle top on the side of his coffin. I remembered how I would have to wake her before I went to school to find her insensible or comatose in her bedroom. An empty bottle of supermarket own brand vodka just tentatively beyond the reach of a limp hand lolling over the side of the bed.

But I have Photoshopped away other details that do not fit my profile of her. A framed wedding portrait, knocked indignantly on its face upon the dressing table. Yesterday's mascara, or maybe even from the day before, driven down her sallow cheeks by tears. My father's favourite topaz blue shirt still clutched tightly in her other, bloodless hand.

I filled up the pipe and took another gratuitous hit, attempted to smoke away those demons of clarity. Fucking Tommy. Forcing these drugs down my dehydrated throat, up into my travel-swollen brain; then disappearing, as everyone ever did, to leave me all alone with these unwanted epiphanies.

He turned up ten minutes later with Jaffa Cakes.

Dan: Interred

I've never been very good at sleeping. I could always find worse things to do. Even after last night's excesses, I still awoke at an unseemly, early hour. My body clock always springing forward, never wound back. I briefly considered going to see Amber, but thought I might have a better chance at the weekend.

It wouldn't do to come all this way and miss her.

Also, Tommy is working today and he wants to tag along and watch.

I think I liked her abstract period best. Because, in truth, now that I'm here and she's turned figurative I haven't given her too much thought. Contrary to conventional wisdom, things look bigger when they're further away. For now, I am overly preoccupied with matters back home. Let me consider this slowly, just to bring myself up to speed.

These are the facts. I don't know if they're true or not:

In the portentous setting of the graveyard, within metres of his remains, my mother told me that it had been my father's choice to go back into the pit. That she had begged him not to do it. That he couldn't stop himself.

"Just like you," she said. "Always had to be moving."

But he's not moving any more, I thought. I looked across at his headstone, the same way a Laotian junk boat skipper once instructed me to turn towards land to quell feelings of sea-sickness.

She told me that he had grown restless in his new desk job, stifled by the breathable air up top. The last thing he wanted was an office with a view, to watch his former comrades emerging every day, with their tribulations and treasures smeared all over their faces. He found himself drawn irrevocably back towards darkness, as all of our family unit have been at one time or another.

Ten months later, he was dead.

Family unknit.

"I couldn't even look at you after he died," she said. "You looked so much like him. You still do, Danny. But now I like it."

Timing is everything, Mother.

Women, burying their children. After her son's death, my Grandma had no time to grieve, instead monitoring her daughter-in-law's own, different descent. She repeatedly offered help and support that was rebuffed. Growing concerned for my welfare, she contacted Social Services with a view to winning custody of me. The case gathered momentum rapidly after my mother threw a Tivo player at the head of a visiting social worker. Fucking Tivo. How fitting an emblem of our failure to adapt. She scored a direct hit and a following report that deemed her "unfit to cope".

Me in the middle. Two women, each tugging at me from either side. Both of them lost their grip momentarily and I fell. Into my very own pit. Just as the move was almost finalised, my Grandma had an accident and was hospitalised for a lengthy period of time. After that, she too was considered unable to care for me. Chaos theory: a woman slips on black ice in a small Yorkshire town, a kid slips through the cracks of the system and slides down into foster care. A butterfly in Tokyo can go fuck itself. Too young to be left on my own and too old to be lovable, I became the gnarled old mongrel of the dog pound, snarling at all who come near.

When I finally bit, the sound of my foster parent's screams sang louder than four years of my Grandmother's protests and my mother's silent indifference. I was sent back to the only family that would tolerate me; my own. What was left of it. Four years earlier my Grandmother would have marched down that pathway to the foster home, breaking stride only to close the gate behind her. Country girls can't help themselves when it comes to that. But on the day she picked me up from there, she limply shuffled along those irregular slabs that always reminded me of broken biscuits, looking haunted and harried. Back bent and in slippers for her arches. She still had many more years before her, but the ones behind her had taken their toll.

I remember that day, being excited that she was coming, crestfallen when I saw her condition. I looked down the room to see my nemesis, the incontinent sadist Kenno, also watching her arrive through another window, willing her to fall. I caught his eye and he walked out of the room, muttering to himself and fingering the greying bandages on his hands. It was me that had put them there.

Kenno was two years older than me and two feet taller than everyone. He took whatever he wanted from all of us in the home, though he never seemed to want what he took. He'd steal kids' soft toys and drown them in toilets, sling their pencil cases over walls. A week previously, I had returned to my room to find him down on all fours, rummaging in my chest of drawers. Three of my Action Force figures were already tucked in the elasticated waistband of his mildewed tracksuit bottoms. Not waving, but drowning.

Without thinking, I dashed over and slammed the drawer shut with my knee, trapping Kenno's hands within. Figures computed on a Little Professor calculator detailed a sixty-three percent decrease in crime after this incident. They also gave my probable chance of survival after his bandages came off as eight percent.

Fast forward.

My grandma had a two-week window of lucidity while I was in Africa. She woke up one morning knowing exactly who she was and realising the consequences of everything she'd ever done. What a truly hideous sensation that must be. She ran the nurses like assets, sending them out to track down my mother. It wasn't hard, she wasn't far away. No one ever goes far away where I come from, because far away is way too far. She called my mother to her bedside and apologised for the failings in her administration.

"She said that she'd been wrong to call Social Services," my mother explained. "Said that we should have sorted it out between ourselves. But we've never been much of a family for talking, have we?"

I said nothing.

This afternoon I walked all the way down to the harbour. There I saw the enamelled fangs of the Opera House rising up out of the ground, like the Devil's under-bite. The pervasive light of the afternoon sun formed the plaque that insidiously crept across their smooth contours.

It all looked so hideously beautiful that I just wanted to blow it up.

Amber: An Invitation

We walk out of the restaurant. Or at least Dan does. I'm floating alongside him like a balloon. We go straight back to the hostel, make a swift bee-line for his room. I feel randy from the seafood and the wine. I'm going to show him the True Face of God resides inside my knickers tonight, and then send him out weeping and limping to the airport's Qantas desk in the morning.

A skinny guy looks up from a paperback as we pass the reception desk hurriedly.

"Is your name Amber?" he asks.

"Yeah, it is," I say, overly defensive. He's Australian. We get everywhere like rust. That makes me nervous. I'm wondering if I've been rumbled, or tracked.

"Someone left a message for you," he says. "I tried to leave it with a girl in your room but she said...well, she wasn't making too much sense, eh? She said you'd gone to Nashville with Kenny Rogers."

Then he glances at Dan, to confirm that he is not in fact Kenny Rogers.

"My travel plans changed," I say, taking the note. "Thanks."

Please don't let it be Neville. Please don't let it be Neville.

I open it anxiously.

"Everything okay?" Dan asks.

"Fine," I say, exhaling in relief. "Some of the people from my trip have arrived. They're saying they'll be up in the bar if I want to come along. Fancy going up?"

"Yeah, sure, if you want to," he replies. I can tell that means that he doesn't. It's the first time I've ever known him to be anything less than honest with me, but I lov...Edit: *I like* him all the more for considering what I want.

"We'll just say a quick hello. What's the worst that could happen in five minutes?"

He shrugs, and we head up.

Dan: This is Manly

I awoke early again. I sat out in the backyard, my usual spot already. Muster point, designated smouldering area. I lost myself in newly found thoughts, until Tommy cuffed me around the back of the head and pulled up a chair. Amicable aggression, always my preferred form of tactility.

"D-Day, eh?" he said, fishing up an oyster of phlegm, shucking it over the neighbour's lattice fence.

"Yep."

Saturday. Tommy had agreed to turn his phone off and let Sydney's kitchens flood. There was no research to undertake. I already had Amber's address, had it all along. It was still where she wrote it, there in the back of my travel journal with a parting message, an obituary of our time together. Call anytime! That's how it ended, how we ended. That's what she scribbled beneath the address, dotting the 'i' with a faithless love heart, an organ in transit that burst in its ice-packed Styrofoam box on the plane ride home.

Oh, I will, Amber.

"Have you thought about what you're going to say to her?" asked Tommy.

"Not really," I replied blankly, sensing his excitement, unwilling to smother it like a chip-pan fire with my newfound *ennui*.

"Shouldn't worry about it too much," he said. "See that washing line?"

It was hard to miss, consuming as it did one half of the tiny yard. It was one of those Y-shaped rotary abortions, like a ham radio aerial that picks up static cling. The same kind our old dog Sabre used to hang from with the tea towel in his jaws.

"Australian invention, that…" said Tommy. "Know what else they invented?"

I shook my head.

"Fuck all!" he said, laughing, rummaging in his pocket for something. "You don't need to worry about what you say to her. We baffled these people with cricket, same as we did all the other colonials. Chucked a couple of pieces of wood and a ball at 'em, then pissed off with all their natural resources. Left 'em scratching their knackers and trying to figure out the rules."

That theory didn't make any kind of sense to me, being as how the colonials were English. But its lazy, unqualified xenophobia appealed to me, at least. Maybe Tommy had been spending too much time drinking with all those disgruntled former skinhead ex-pats in English bars with red phone boxes in the snug.

"There was only America where it didn't take," he added as an afterthought, as if that suddenly pulled it into focus kaleidoscopically.

He extricated the little hash pipe and began loading it with his expectations. It looked tiny in his grasp, like a Stoner Barbie accessory.

"And if she doesn't pay we'll just smash her windows and leg it," he mused, after a while.

So, we had a plan.

"Do you even like it here, Tommy?" I asked my oldest friend.

He sparked up the pipe and his words rode out of the resulting smoke as a louche dragon on the fog:

"I bastard love it, Dan," he chuckled.

I abstained from the pot myself, my head fogged over enough already. After breakfast and a shower, Tommy insisted he was safe to drive, and indeed, he piloted the van a lot more cautiously than he had on the airport pick-up. We arrived at Manly Beach in the latter part of the morning and flukily found a parking spot being vacated by an atrophied muscle car just as we rounded the corner onto the seafront.

"The stars are aligning themselves correctly," posited Tommy. Maybe still a little stoned, then. Always hard to tell with him.

I surveyed the beautiful abattoir of the beach bodies, found my eyes drawn to one solitary figure amidst the masses. He was sat next to his own surfboard, stuffed upright into the shifting earth as both a totem and a Freudian statement of intent. His name probably ended with a vowel. He had a beer in his hand already, even though when it made him belch he could probably taste eggy-bread. He was waiting to be discovered, as we all are, glancing across at a group of girls who were oblivious to his existence. They were lazily busy pouring themselves into lifestyle magazines and Jodi Picoult novels, transferring their DNA into the text through lightly greased fingerprints.

He tried to remain serene and Zen-like, but would blow his composure once in a while, violently flicking the accumulating sand on his feet, as though it had lunged at him unexpectedly.

Away from the water, previously bored sorts had donned board-shorts and now prowled the boardwalk. Scoping out the beach bunnies, who flicked their tails at them dismissively. Meanwhile, roller-bladers cut through all the tightly gathered flesh like cosmetic surgeons' scalpels.

It reminded me of my extended stay in Venice Beach, when I tended to my sick Brazilian friend Fabio. I thought then about how I had never accepted his offer to stay with him in Rio. A flight there would have cost roughly the same as my flight to Sydney. Negotiating the favelas of that city would have been child's play after the time I have wasted attempting to gain access to the shady chambers of Amber's darkened heart.

"This is her street," I exclaimed, my eyes moving from the journal address to a road sign and back again. "That must be her building, right over..."

There.

I thought maybe she'd be a couple of roads back, but there it was, right by the waterfront. Nice building. Stucco, pastel painted. She'd clearly done very well for herself.

"Her drainpipes need gutting," said Tommy.

At first, I took that to be some kind of vague threat, or sexual euphemism. I wasn't really listening. I was coming around then, picking up her scent on the sea breeze:

"Apartment 313, that's probably the third floor, eh?"

"We'd need to be keen shots to break those windows," Tommy put in. "Feels like we're on a stakeout. We should get some doughnuts."

A gangly young lad walked past the car, carrying a cluster of helium balloons that would surely have divorced him from the ground were it not for the vending tray he wore as ballast.

"Hey, nipper!" Tommy shouted. "What you flogging?"

The kid clearly had no idea what Tommy was saying, but mooched over toward the van anyway. From his low angle, Tommy tried to peer up his wares.

"What you selling, kid?"

"Balloons," he said.

He looked like he'd been born tanned, dropped on that beach some thirteen years ago like a fumbled Hackensack, sheathed in placenta that reeked of Hawaiian Tropic.

"What you got in the tray, then, young 'un?" Tommy asked. "Anything nice? Any chocolate?"

The lad stared down at the tray like he was memorizing its contents for Kim's Game.

"Balloon accessories," he said, finally, done with his inventory.

"Balloon accessories?" Tommy asked, winking across at me.

"String, mostly," he concluded, after another lengthy study.

"Ah, just gimme a balloon then."

"Which one do you want?" the kid enquired.

"Tell you what, mate, you choose," said Tommy, clearly growing tired of the exchange then, the lad's blunt wit being sharper than he expected. "You're obviously a leading authority in the field."

The boy picked the most incongruous balloon he could find and handed it to Tommy with relish, who coughed up his money without concern. It was cerise, with a picture of a unicorn on the front. I watched Tommy inspecting it delightedly and considered how, given his parentage, he might have developed an understandable aversion to anything vaguely fairground related. Considered broaching this topic to him, saw him shaking the balloon between his gargantuan hands, thought again.

"It's got glitter in it," he said, by way of explanation.

I looked at the now stationary orb and saw tiny intimations of silver, cascading down through the balloon's interior like falling stars.

All the people I met on my travels were the stars that I navigated by. At our varied points of departure, they offered up their continued friendship to me and I swatted them away like Louisiana lightning bugs. When I returned home, the nights were much darker without them. But all the stars are really just floodlit tombstones, moratoriums for deceased light. They did not align themselves correctly as far as Amber and I were concerned. The Great Bear got sarcoptic mange, The Plough got stuck in a furrow, and The Big Dipper plummeted from the sky like The Big Bopper.

She's a black hole now, but I found myself peering in one last time.

I looked back at the windows on the third floor, just in time to see one opening, some kind of smoke emerging from it. When it dissipated, I saw Amber's face. She'd been straining pasta at the sink, opening the window to let out the steam. Spaghetti, I knew. She looked beautiful then, her hair a little longer, maybe even a shade darker. Perhaps just still a little wet from the shower. Smiling benignly, looking off into the distance, gazing out to the kite-surfers on the water. Until the tea towel slipped and her delicate hand connected against the hot steel of the colander.

She was on the other side of the world once. Then she was on the other side of the street. I watched her burn briefly, with more satisfaction than was seemly. I thought it was the first time I had ever seen her look startled.

Then I remembered that it wasn't. It wasn't even the second. There was that time on the top of Table Mountain. And then, there was that last night in the hostel bar.

Amber: A Rejection

In spite of all my best efforts, in spite of all the brain cells I drown in alcohol, like kittens in a sack, I still somehow keep learning things. Here's something I do know to be true: the first impressions you make about people usually turn out to be way off the mark. Like, when I first met Neville I thought he was sweet as. Like, when I first met Dan I thought he was a bit of a dick.

So now I'm worried, because the people that have turned up for the trip seem really nice. This makes me think that as soon as the bus gets out of the hostel gates their smiles will clatter down onto the road and I'll be doomed to three weeks of travel with a group of maniacs and basic toilet facilities.

At least I won't be alone. But I won't be with the one person I want to be with.

He's not a group person, but I can tell that he's trying. I think of my dog Benchy, his restlessness and his low growl when the sound of fireworks came hurtling across from the harbour. We're seated in one of the hostel bar's bigger booths and both Dan and I keep glancing across to the smaller one we shared previously. It's empty, as it should always be from now on. It was our Commonwealth. But we're still together, for the moment at least: his thumb is wedged down into the belt loop of my dress and my hand is resting on his hot thigh. I'd swear I can feel his pulse, though as a nurse I know that's not really possible. Not unless I snake my hand up the loose leg of his shorts towards his femoral artery. Probably inappropriate, being as we're in company. Later, Amber. But I can feel it. It's beating fast. I instinctively glance toward my lapel to time it against my fob watch.

I'm not wearing the fob watch. I have no lapel. We're still together, but we're flanked by the people who will take me away from him. Two excitable girls from New Zealand are at my side and, for the moment, they're thankfully talking to each other. Dan has this Irish guy called Eamonn next to him, drunk and a bit lairy, bucking all stereotypes, chewing his ear off. If you could invent a character you'd least like to see Dan seated next to he'd be the dead spit of Eamonn. I nestle closer to hear what they're saying, offer back-up if required.

"So, you'll be looking forward to the trip then, Dan?" he asks.

"I'm not going on the trip, Eamonn," explains Dan, tersely. "I already told you that two minutes ago."

"Ah, right, so the two of youse..." He points at the both of us with a wagging finger. "The two of youse aren't...."

"We *are*," I interject, leaning across Dan, feeling the heat he's kicking out. "We are. But Dan's not going on the trip. That's all."

"Jeez, you must be some trusting soul, Dan, leaving a girl like that to her own devices!"

I don't know what he means when he calls me a 'girl like that', but I don't care. Dan doesn't respond, because he's not listening. We're looking at each other again now, and everyone else in the room just flew out of the windows. He rests his forehead against mine and I take his face in my hands. It's smooth to the touch, because he shaved to look nice for dinner, because he shaved to look nice for me.

"How're you doing?" he asks, softly.

"Alright. How're you?"

He shrugs with his eyebrows.

"Want to get out of here?"

He nods. He's been rendered mute from all this loud talk. I drain my glass of wine and start to gather my things.

"Just got to get some ciggies," I say.

"I'll get them for you," he offers. "I need to move. You say your goodbyes to everyone and I'll meet you by the door."

"Okay, thanks."

He taps Eamonn, who's trying to crack onto some girl next to him, on the shoulder and slips past him out of the booth. Eamonn immediately jettisons the chick and moves over to where I'm sat. He moves as though he's on casters. He starts talking to me, but it's just like that tour guide at Robben Island or that teacher from Charlie Brown again. I'm not listening. I'm watching my man.

He's been feeding rand notes into the cigarette machine, but it keeps spitting the last one out. I smile to myself as I watch him repeatedly smooth it out and push it in the slot again. And again. And again. Now he's holding the note up to the dim light and inspecting it. A barman comes over and offers him another one, but I see Dan shake his head and wave him away. The barman shrugs and leaves, shaking his own head as he turns back toward another customer.

He's leaning his head against the Perspex at the front of the machine now. He's not even looking at what he's doing any more; just feeding the money into the slot, keeping his hand there and forcing it right back in as soon as it rejects it. I'm not sure if he's aware of it, but his head is starting to bob rhythmically to mirror the movement. I feel like I'm filming a nature documentary, recording life's routine savagery, wondering whether I should intervene. I fish in my *clutch* bag for more change and raise myself to my feet.

I walk towards him, still smiling, but not for long. As I get closer, I'm horrified to see that he is now butting his head against the front of the cigarette machine. I'm reminded of those wasps at the end of summer, drunk on rotten fruit, banging their antennae against my flat's window. Again. And again. He doesn't even stop when the Perspex cracks. I call out his name and he doesn't hear me, even though I'm stood right next to him now. By the third time, I'm shouting it, with tears in my eyes. He finally spins around, toward me and the bank note I'm holding out in a trembling hand.

He looks right at me and right through me. He's in one of those frugal states, or whatever they're called. I've never seen so much anger burning through a man. His arms suddenly seem bigger, seem like they could crush me. He's familiar but he looks like a stranger. He's someone I used to know or thought I knew or never knew. I love him and he terrifies me. I know now that he could hurt me. I can't have that, just can't have that in my life again. Not so soon after Neville. Not now. Not ever.

First impressions and last impressions. I've learned nothing, and the truth is a pack of lies. There was a word that Dan used once. Recidivist. I didn't know what it meant, so I looked it up in a dictionary at the hostel's book exchange. I know what it means now. I'll take care of Dan tonight, because that's what I'm trained to do. But I'm leaving Cape Town tomorrow.

He stays here.

Dan: Catch and Release

I woke up alone in Cape Town, in a queen-sized bed whose matriarch had abdicated. I woke up alone with yet another unqualified lump on my head, and no idea how it got there. I remember everything about all the people who hurt me and all the ways they did it. How much have I forgotten about all the ways I hurt *them*?

Back at the beach, I stared up at the open window for a long time, but she never reappeared. The clearing condensation on the glass dripped away like tears. When I finally looked over at Tommy, he was rubbing the balloon against his T-shirt, trying to generate a static charge that would make it stick. Catching me regarding him, he flushed and shrugged awkwardly.

"Don't know what to do with it now I've got it," he said.

I looked back toward the third floor one last time.

"Let it go," I replied, sighing.

He did. The balloon wobbled as it exited the car. Buffeted by a sudden bluster of wind from the sea that thrilled and almost killed four kite-surfers, it was sent careening sideways, over towards Amber's side of the street. Once there, and with the wind now died away, the unicorn rose up and up, on an unmanned mission to puncture the very epicentre of the cloudless, azure sky with its horn.

It rode right past her window, and she didn't even see it.

"We're not going are we?" Tommy asked. "Have you bottled it? Are we going?"

I said nothing; because sometimes that's all that needs to be said. He sighed and released the handbrake, uncoupled us from the tarmac.

"At least tell me *where* we're going."

"Home," I said.

"We came all this way," Tommy commented, gunning the ignition on the van. "And I didn't even get a fucking ice-cream."

Dan: Gay Breast Milk

I returned from Sydney about a month ago. While I was there, Tommy's girlfriend never came back or even contacted him. Sometimes they don't. Sometimes I think the word "goodbye" has been stricken from our language forever. Everyone just hangs up, like they do on the phones in American movies. But who am I to talk? I left someone for dead once, too.

The best day I had during my time there was when Tommy and I went out with his neighbours, a nice couple called Carter and Nathan. Two colourful, larger than life characters who fit together like Duplo bricks. Carter is what is known in gay terminology as a "bear" – a big, hairy man with a proclivity for raiding other men's picnic areas. That is, he was, until he met the love of his life. Nathan is smaller, cut up like a washboard, waxed up like a surfboard. I don't know what the word is for one of his ilk. A "Boo-Boo" maybe, a Park Ranger, a honeypot, a scratching tree...

They approached Tommy regarding the spittle found on their patio's seraphim figures, which he thoughtfully blamed on me and my lack of class. The conversation finished up amicably with an invitation to a day out on their boat, the sole proviso being that I didn't spit on it.

So, on a beautiful summer's day in Sydney, we walked briskly past the breeders loitering around the harbour in their woefully uncoordinated clothes and headed out over the water to Watson's Bay. We dined on fish and chips, from the famous Doyle's restaurant by the beach. The real men drank beer and I took a banana milkshake. Carter draped himself around his partner like a fur stole. He fed Nathan chips periodically as though he were a baby bird. I looked at Tommy seated next to me on the bench and felt like putting an arm around him, if only for symmetry. The pair of them emitted so much dazzling love that we had to keep our sunglasses on in the shade.

"So what you doing here, Dan?" Nathan asked me during our meal. "Just came over to see your mate, eh?"

I glanced at Tommy, who was grinning at me and doing something suggestive with a saveloy under the table, out of sight of the other two.

"I wouldn't come all this way to see an enemy," I said, sounding oddly Jewish, breaking down my Golem. I took a sip of my milkshake and waited for the conversation to move on.

"How come you don't drink?" Carter asked.

Not the direction I had hoped for.

"My mo..." I thought for a second, frowned. "My mum won't let me."

"Aw, fuck her! My mum hasn't spoken to me since I came out," he said. "Now everything she disapproves of I do twice as hard. If you'll excuse the..."

"Excused," said Tommy quickly.

"You haven't spent much time with gay people, have you Tommy?" Nathan, the muse, mused.

"Just Dan, really," said Tommy, beaming.

"Dan's not gay!" Carter exclaimed. "Look at his haircut!"

"Wanna try?" I asked Carter, proffering my milkshake as a bribe to steer the conversation around and away from my head.

"No thanks," he replied, and then muttered something I couldn't quite catch.

"Sorry," I said. "But did you just say you were lactating tomorrow?"

"I said that I'm lactose intolerant," he replied, laughing.

"You really don't know much about gay people, do you, Dan?" Tommy goaded. "They don't produce breast milk."

I laughed but I was wondering if it was all somehow linked. Carter's homosexuality, his mother's rejection of him, his own body's rejection of maternal milk. Like how lesbians favour cats over dogs and name them after feisty heroines.

Unfortunately, just as we were finishing our meal, the clouds rolled abruptly in and it began to rain. We retreated beneath the canopy of the boat and remained there, with the boys drinking for the rest of the day. It was only when the eskie was getting dangerously close to empty that we finally elected to return to the mainland.

As we approached the harbour, our skipper Carter had to go below deck to "the little girl's room."

How winsome.

He instructed me to take the ship's helm in his absence. I approached the fore hesitantly, but as soon as I laid my sweaty palms on the wheel, I had an epiphany. The first few days of my trip had all been a bit of a blur and hard to take in, but in that moment I had the stark realisation that I, a humble manual labourer from a dulled penny of a Northern town, was now at the other side of the world and currently piloting a large motor cruiser. Heading back towards Sydney Opera House in the dwindling light once more, but I saw it a little differently this time around, as flags guiding me back in to where I needed to be. I put my flip-flopped foot flat to the pedal and the resulting spray on my face felt like God herself was blowing me a big, sloppy kiss.

There wasn't a day I was in Sydney that I didn't think about Amber, consider the possibility that I might bump into her in some bar or coffee shop. Spool that scenario out in my head; think about how it might play...

But there was never a day when I did anything to facilitate it, either. I keep banging my head against immobilised objects, but maybe it's me who needs to move.

Dan: Behind the Green Door

Subject to popular demand, and with my customarily impeccable timing, I painted my grandmother's front door. *My door*, now, I suppose. To my house. When done, I dropped my brush in the turps jar and stepped backwards onto the path to take a good look at my handiwork, accidentally bumping into a figure behind me. My mother, who had somehow glided across the lumpy tarmac as though it were ice.

"Sorry, love," she said, as we both collected ourselves and shrank away from each other. She groaned a little as she stooped to pick up a tin of canned goods rolling out of her shopping bag. "Didn't mean to scare you."

"You didn't," I said, as I regained my unsure footing. She did though. She always could. Not because I knew what she was capable of. Rather, because I knew what she was incapable of. I turned to face her, automatically inserting myself between her and the front door.

"It's a nice colour," she offered, up on tiptoes, peeking over my shoulder.

"Green for go," I said.

She glanced at me then. I've spent most of my life looking down on her, but I had never seen her looking so small as she did in that moment. I could see the glaucoma of hurt clouding her eyes. She stared at her feet and rubbed her hands together as though she were trying to wring herself away, back down through the cracked concrete of the path, like reverse rocket salad. My own hand, suddenly possessed, moved impulsively toward her shoulder until I snapped it viciously back into place, making a whip-crack in the air that surprised us both.

The reverse polarity between us is so strong that we can't even control our own bodies when we are around each other. We are antimatter. We are emotional spastics. We were both silent for a long time, until I couldn't hold my breath any longer and sighed.

"Did you kick your ball in my yard again?" I asked her.

She looked up at me with an almost-smile. I too, thought maybe I smiled back, but for all the dominion I had over my own face it might just have appeared as a terrible leer.

"Let's get this over with," I mumbled. Then I took a deep breath and turned awkwardly back toward the door, regarded the cooling brush-strokes once more, and stepped through it.

I didn't close it behind me.

Couldn't. The paint was still drying.

I stood a good, safe distance inside the living room and braced myself for her arrival.

Dan: All Fingers and Thumbs and Trunks

I stood there, inert, for a good five minutes. Or maybe it was two minutes. Maybe it was even thirty seconds. She didn't follow. Maddened, I tramped back to the front door, found her still nailed to the spot I had left her in.

"Was that, like…too oblique for you?" I asked. "I thought you were coming in."

"Well, I didn't know what was going on," she retorted, indignantly. "You just mumbled summat and ran off."

My mother, the vampire. She has to wait to be invited over the threshold. Accordingly, I motioned toward the doorway in an exaggerated fashion, like some demented air steward.

"Watch the paintwork," I said, as she shuffled past me.

"Yeah, I know, Dan. I just saw you with a brush in your hand, for God's sake."

She stepped into the living room before me. She was still clutching her plastic shopping bag, her knuckles whitening on the handles as though she were a chameleon.

"It hasn't changed much, from what I remember," she said, scanning the room. "I can still see your Grandma everywhere in here."

I looked around the place, tried to see it through her eyes. And failed. The only thing I could see in that room was the one thing she couldn't, the one thing that wasn't supposed to be there.

"Alright, listen," I said, resignedly. "If you've got any ideas, let's have 'em. Cos I haven't got a clue what we're supposed to do now."

"Well...I dunno," she began. "What about a drink?"

She must have seen the distress flare that went off behind my eyes at that last word.

"Coffee?" she added.

"Right."

Two-up, two-down. It's a small house, getting smaller all the time. Six rapid paces took me away from her and through to the kitchen. I filled the kettle with trembling hands, then splayed them on the worktop to steady myself. I looked beyond paint-flecked fingers and fixated upon the rambunctious old kettle as it began its familiar anti-circadian rhythm. I felt better there, my foot tapping against the tiles, almost a universe away from the Black Hole sucking up the Axminster.

"I...I came around once before. To see how you were doing after the..." she called, falteringly, through the void. "I saw Bert. He said you were off on your travels again."

"Australia," I said. Stupidly nodding, even though I was in another room.

"Haven't you been there before?" she asked. "I always thought you never went to the same place twice."

"I went to see someone," I said, pausing. "Tommy."

"Oh, that's nice! I forgot he was over there. How's he doing? Has he settled down?"

"I wouldn't exactly say that," I replied, almost laughing.

"No," she said. "I suppose not."

That old adage about a watched pot never boiling, it's a load of bollocks. I stuck my head into the rattling kettle's steam for as long as I could stand to, hoping maybe I would reappear in Brigadoon. She could have at least asked for tea; that would have bought me a little more time as I let the bag steep.

"How do you take it?" I shouted through to the living room, too loudly, pretending that I didn't know.

"Just milk, love. No sugar."

I swear to Christ, if she'd have said she was sweet enough already, I would've gouged her tongue out with the spoon.

I walked back into the living room, trying to tread heavily to muffle the sounds of the mugs rattling in my unsteady hands. She had her back to me, fiddling about with something on the windowsill that I couldn't see. I quickly posited the mugs on the table, slopping hot coffee as I did so.

"What're you doing?" I asked, alarmed, moving towards her hurriedly.

It was the smallest soapstone elephant, one of the family of three I had bought my Grandma from a market stall outside the Red Fort in Delhi. I jemmied it from her hands and set it back on the ledge, back to the same small, dust-free spot it had resided in for the last eight years.

"Ow, Dan," she cried. "Jesus!"

"Sorry," I muttered. "But you shouldn't go touching things that don't belong to you."

"I was just turning them to face the window," she offered. She herself had turned away from me petulantly, with one hand cupped around the fingers of the other, as though I had broken them. "For good luck."

"Aren't we blessed enough already?" I asked, giving out a long sigh.

Dan: The Glossy Finish

There's that feeling you get with shoelaces. You stoop to tie up the one on the left, but then end up re-tying the one on the right too, just because it feels slack by comparison. Once I start something I can't stop. I only intended to paint the front door, but as soon as I prised open the first Dulux I was an addict. Now there are so many tins of emulsion in play that the house looks like a staging of *Stomp*.

A Swedish hippy I encountered in Belize once told me that paint smells like the future.

"How would you know that?" I asked him.

He was right, though. Maybe it's just the fumes, but there are visions in those tins. The whole house is a work in progress now. I've been racing to get everything finished before I start my new job in two weeks' time. It's just some crappy minimum wage warehouse position; I'm not entirely sure what the work entails. I'll probably be opening boxes, or closing boxes, or filling boxes, or emptying boxes, or making boxes, or destroying boxes. Closing boxes might be the biggest challenge for me. Like any other form of employment, it will soon no doubt become the newfound focal point for all my aggression and disdain. We all need that though, it's no coincidence that the spleen is shaped like a fist. I can't say that I'm looking forward to it too much.

Although I am.

My mother has a similarly addictive personality. We are finding new ways to yoke our shared traits. She calls around occasionally, was here only yesterday. She's quite a good decorator. The first few times she visited, it was fairly awkward. My most abiding memory of those initial meetings is the clanking of teaspoons against cups, pealing out the campanology of discomfort, peeling the skin off the silence.

The third time she came, I was stripping wallpaper and she just took her coat straight off and pitched in, while I studied her from my vantage point on the stepladder like a tin-pot god.

"Could I borrow an old shirt?" she asked, after a while. "Mine's getting mucky."

"I know just the very thing," I said.

I went upstairs, into my room, and took my father's topaz blue shirt out of the bedside cabinet.

I was halfway down the stairs with it before I changed my mind, folded it up like a funeral flag and returned it to the drawer. Selected instead a worn-out T-shirt from a pile in the laundry basket and headed back into the living room. That was me acquiescing, aquaplaning and skidding to a halt.

I find it easier talking to her when we are engaged in these chores, there being much less eye contact to avoid. Maybe she'll evaporate like the turpentine fumes once it's finished. Maybe she'll even drink the turpentine. But for now, she's clean, sober and a reasonably skilled grouter. I might like her a little bit. It seems important to like her now, so that I can hate her all the more when she disappears again.

Luckily, she didn't call around the day I was cleaning up the bottom of the yard. I found a dead animal round the back of an overgrown gooseberry bush, a grotty subversion of one of the more feasible creation myths. It wasn't the ginger tom. It was a black cat. Not so lucky, after all, not when it crossed my path. I could sense it had once been insouciant, pictured it sashaying along a narrow fence top for no other reason than to compound the failings of a watching dog. Now, it was decomposing badly, with maggots knitting themselves together into a modesty shawl to cover its exposed and chewed away flesh. Its tongue was lolling obscenely out of its mouth in a manner that reminded me of my backpack, Patty Hearst, when I found her ransacked at Dubai Airport.

Heartbreakingly, the cat wore a blue felt collar studded with diamante stars. There was no name-tag attached, but I knew that her name was Duffy. I knew this because I had seen her image on a 'Missing' poster in the window of the corner shop. I could envisage some little girl in a pink coat and pigtails being pushed gently towards the counter by her mother. Then shyly proffering the poster to Mr Singh, looking up at his silvery explosions of nasal hair like a firework display as he accepted it and smiled kindly down at her.

I sat next to the decaying form and wept. Poor little bastard. Somebody loved that cat and I killed it. Yet another example of my anger being posted to all the wrong addresses.

As for Patty Hearst herself, she has returned to her closet. I stood at the baggage carousel in Heathrow one last time and she, at least, came back to me. I don't think she'll be travelling again for a while. I've got work to do here.

Last night, after gutting the bathroom, my mother and I dusted down two old, striped deckchairs from the shed and sat out on the newly trimmed lawn. I didn't mention that Bert's wife died in one of them, that he had passed them onto my Grandmother and they had been in storage ever since. We drank coffee, just like we always do now. My mother is still reacquainting herself with hot beverages.

"Will you keep the house on, Dan?" she asked, blowing steam from her mug. "Will you stay?"

"I guess so," I replied, after thinking about it for a while. "I haven't got anywhere else to go."

"That's a first," she said. "For you."

It was a mild evening given the time of year. We looked out over the back fields of ragwort and rapeseed, then past the canal full of dead puppies and the towpath where the gypsies tether their ponies, to fatten them up for the glue factory. We watched a brilliant, blood orange sun squeeze itself into the grey cooling towers of the nearby power station. The amenable silence we shared together was punctured only by the low wail of a distant siren, another police car heading through the estate.

Why would I think about going anywhere when there's all this beauty here?

"New beginnings," my mother said, sighing.

I almost vomited a little in my coffee mug. We're not at the stage for that kind of talk, perhaps never will be. The future is a tin we haven't opened yet. For now, we're still painting over the past.

But it seemed like I'd misunderstood her once again. When I turned to regard her, she was pointing towards the soil border at the edge of the lawn. I followed the direction of her extended finger. There I saw the first snowdrops of winter, still wet behind the ears, all wobbly heads with soft fontanelles, unsteadily pushing their way up through the dark earth.

I didn't dare tell her that was where I'd buried the cat.

If you enjoyed this title, follow Obliterati Press on Twitter and Facebook for details of forthcoming releases.

@ObliteratiPress

https://www.facebook.com/ObliteratiPress

Also, be sure to check out our website for regular short story contributions.

Also available from Obliterati Press:

LORD OF THE DEAD

By

Richard Rippon

A woman's body has been found on the moors of Northumberland, brutally murdered and dismembered. Northumbria police enlist the help of unconventional psychologist Jon Atherton, a decision complicated by his personal history with lead investigator Detective Sergeant Kate Prejean.

As Christmas approaches and pressure mounts on the force, Prejean and Atherton's personal lives begin to unravel as they find themselves the focus of media attention, and that of the killer known only as Son Of Geb.